THE JUMP

STORIES FOR UNCERTAIN TIMES

THE JUMP

STORIES FOR UNCERTAIN TIMES

PETER A HEMPEL

AARONS PRESS

ISBN number: 978-0-578-54561-5

202-404-27

DEDICATION

I'm very lucky to have two wonderful daughters, Hadley and Holly. My younger daughter, Holly, has read all the stories and has liked all of them; her most common reaction is, "That's really funny." My older daughter, Hadley, has read some of the stories; she approaches my stories cautiously and finds them, "well written, but pretty dark."

In that spirit, I would like to dedicate this book to my daughters with all my love and best wishes.

"In this vale of tears, it is temptingly easy to conclude that our too-brief life is but a cruel irony, a lingering death sentence with no hope and little consolation."

Peter A Hempel
[University of Texas at Austin]

Table of Contents

CREDITS AND NOTES

"Rudolph at Rest – A Christmas Story" was originally published in the December 2016 issue of *The Echo* magazine (Princeton, NJ). It was subsequently posted on their website:

https://communitynews.org/2016/11/28/rudolph-at-rest-a-christmas-story /

"Meine Yiddische Barbie" was published online by *Red Fez* magazine, Issue 108 (January 2018):

https://www.redfez.net/fiction/jewish-meine-yiddische-barbie-876/99

"Schrödinger's Girl" was published December 5, 2016, by *Every Day Fiction* (a flash fiction website):

https://everydayfiction.com/schrodingers-girl-by-peter-a-hempel/

(The version printed here restores two cuts that were made for the online version.)

"Motorcycle Ken Weeps" was published by *Vestal Review* as part of its "18x18 Contest" for stories with 18 letters in their titles and 18 words in the story (it came in 2nd in the reader voting):

http://www.vestalreview.org/motorcycle-ken-weeps/

"**Icarus and the Butterflies**" is the full version of the "Butterflies" story the narrator plagiarizes from a [fictitious] literary magazine, *Oestrus Rising*, in "Telling Stories"

"**The Night of the Chimps**" *Content warning*: when I submitted an earlier version of this story to an online journal, the editor replied with an extensive email, which began, "Your story made the rounds here quickly, producing voluminous discussion." To me, this sounded like a good sign—the kind of thing you like to hear, that your material is thought-provoking and discussion-worthy. From there however, the editor proceeded to insult me, my intelligence, my writing, and ended with this note: "*Please understand that none of our editors or audience will tolerate your work here.*"

On the other hand, some of the people who have read this story rate it as one of their favorites. I have added some material at the end in the version in this collection to give it a slightly more moralistic tone, since irony oft wings by audiences (and editors) these days. Nonetheless, sensitive readers may wish to scurry past this story with eyes shut tight.

I.

EXCURSIONS INTO THE UNCERTAIN

A QUESTION FOR THE RABBI

THE FIRST TIME Aaron noticed anything was when he was putting on his running shoes for an early morning jog. There was a spot on the top of his left foot that seemed slightly swollen and was definitely itchy. Aaron wasn't one to be an alarmist about such things, so he just laced up and headed out for his run.

Aaron Stiegler was 35 and had gotten into running a few years ago. Last year he had done his first marathon, and was planning to do another one sometime this coming fall. This morning he went out to Prospect Park to run his usual route—slightly over seven miles at roughly an eight-minute pace. It was a beautiful spring morning in Brooklyn, warm and sunny with a few small white clouds adding contrast to the bright blue sky. He loved being out in nature, with the trees and the green spaces and the feeling of being wholly removed from city life.

When he got back to his apartment, his wife, Vicki, was just leaving for work and gave him a passing peck on the cheek on her way out the door. Vicki had a high-powered job at one of the big consulting firms in Manhattan and worked long hours; Aaron was an illustrator at a fashion magazine here in

Brooklyn—it was a full-time job, but much more re-laxed and life-friendly.

Aaron went in and took off his running gear and was about to hop into the shower to rinse off after his run. He looked down at his foot and saw that the spot he had noticed earlier was still there, and might even have been a bit redder and more swollen than before. It certainly had not stopped being itchy. Maybe the run had irritated it. Be that as it may, he was on the verge of being late for work, so he finished his shower in a hurry and got dressed and headed for the subway.

When he got home that evening, the day had been busy enough that he had pretty much forgotten about his foot, but now he was noticing it again, and it was getting worse. Fuck it. For dinner, Vicki, who had got-ten home after seven as usual, had ordered in Chinese, which was a big help because it meant he didn't have to figure out how to put on shoes with his foot acting up like this. After dinner, Aaron popped two Advil to help him sleep through it.

* * *

Next morning, Vicki got up earlier than usual for an early-morning conference call at her office. "Don't sleep too late," she reminded him as she left for work.

At 9:30, way past time to be at his office, Aaron was still lying in bed. His foot was hurting like hell now, but he didn't want to pull the bed sheets off and actu-ally see what it looked like. He had to of course, and when he did, he nearly freaked out. The spot had got-ten way redder, the center of it was pushing up and, in the middle, there was an area that looked almost green.

No more Advil. He needed to do something. He called his doctor's office, not really expecting to be able to see him on short notice but also not wanting to have to go to the ER. He was in luck. Another patient had canceled and Dr. Levine could see him in a half hour. Aaron quickly threw on some clothes and called an Uber to take him to Dr. Levine's office. His clothes were no problem, but there was no kind of shoe that was going to work for his foot in this shape. He wrapped a towel around his left foot and tied it loosely with the sash from his bathrobe, and put the left shoe in a paper bag to take with him. When the Uber arrived, Aaron limped awkwardly down the stairs and hopped in, wincing in pain as he did so. "Geez buddy, you okay?" asked the driver.

As they drove, the pain was getting more intense, and suddenly Aaron felt something burst or pop or something under the towel. He had no desire to look and see what had happened.

Just climbing the few stairs to get up to Dr. Levine's office was brutal. But at least he was somewhere where he could finally get this damn thing taken care of.

It'd taken him nearly 30 minutes just to get to the office, so Dr. Levine was able to see him almost immediately. Dr. Levine was in his 40s; he had learned from old-school doctors who believed in the importance of a personal connection with their patients, but he was young enough to be very new school when it came to checking things out and running tests. When Aaron took a seat in his office, Dr. Levine saw the towel wrapped around his foot. "So, Aaron, what's going on with your foot?" he asked. "Let's take a look."

Gingerly and reluctantly, Aaron unwrapped the towel. He didn't really want to look, he just wanted the doctor to see it. "Oh my God," said the doctor. "What the hell *happened* here? And what the hell is *that*?"

Aaron turned and looked at his foot for the first time since the towel had come off. What he saw was not just the inflamed red spot, but now there was something green sticking out. It looked like the shoot of some kind of plant. As the two men watched, the shoot unfurled and opened up, with a small leaf on either side. "What the...?" said Dr. Levine.

Aaron felt like he wanted to just pass out and not have to deal with any of this. He wanted it to all just be some kind of goddamn dream. But, of course, it wasn't.

* * *

Dr. Levine continued staring at it. "Maybe we should just cut it off and do a biopsy," he suggested. He got a pair of scissors and snipped at the base of the shoot.

Aaron screamed. The pain before was nothing like this. He was in total agony. Dr. Levine called his nurse, and told her to bring one of the morphine syringes from the locked medicine cabinet. Fast.

When the nurse came in with the syringe, Dr. Levine injected it in Aaron's arm immediately. "I'm terribly sorry," he said. "I had no idea this would happen. We need to get you to the hospital."

The morphine helped, but Aaron's foot was still hurting a lot. Dr. Levine had his nurse get his car and bring it around front. He helped Aaron down the stairs and put him in the passenger seat, and then got into the driver's seat. "I didn't want you to have to go through all the usual ER admissions crap, so I'm taking you over personally."

When they got to the hospital, Dr. Levine talked with the head nurse and told her the tests that he wanted run. He needed the results ASAP. He told Aaron he would be back when they had the results from the tests.

First, of course, blood tests. Then a bunch of X-rays. And then an MRI scan. Fortunately, Aaron was still woozy from the morphine, so the pain seemed to be coming at him from a distance. After the MRI was completed, the nurse had Aaron transferred to a private room while they waited for the results.

It took about three hours, during which Aaron managed to doze and forget about everything until Dr. Levine returned.

* * *

When Dr. Levine arrived, he had another man with him. "Aaron, this is Dr. Hoffmeyer. He's a botanical scientist from the Brooklyn Botanical Gardens. I asked him to come in to see if he could help us figure out what's going on here."

"Pleased to meet you Mr. Stiegler," said Dr. Hoffmeyer, and shook Aaron's hand. "I've been looking at your lab work, and I must say it's quite confusing. Do you eat a lot of apples?"

"Apples?" said Aaron. "Not really. I'm not really a big fan of apples. Usually only if somebody leaves some around in a bowl in the break room at work."

"When would you say was the last time you had an apple?"

"I don't know, maybe a week ago or more. Someone had brought some apples into the break room and I ate one. What the hell is going on? Why are you asking me about apples?"

"Well," explained Dr. Hoffmeyer, "the lab did a biopsy on the snippet Dr. Levine cut off this morning. And when they couldn't figure out anything from the standard analyses, and since it looked like a plant, they sent it over to the Botanical Gardens to see if we could figure it out. And what it looks like is the sprout of an apple tree seedling."

"*What?* That doesn't make any sense at all."

"You're right, but nothing about this situation makes any sense at all."

* * *

Dr. Levine held up some X-ray films. "Aaron, we've been looking at these, and it looks as if some kind of plant was growing in your foot. You can see here where a root system was developing. It looks as if it was growing pretty damn fast. You can see how it's wrapped around some of the bones in your foot already. Neither of us has ever seen or heard of anything like this, ever."

"So now what? asked Aaron.

"We're not really sure," said Dr. Levine. "Our best hope is that cutting off the top this morning killed it, but that still leaves the question of what to do with the rest of the root system. What happens next? Will it just dissolve and go away, or will it create some kind of infection? I showed this to the head surgeon and he explained it would be incredibly difficult to remove these roots surgically. Very worst-case—and I emphasize *very* worst-case—if it looks as if it's going to get dangerously infected, we might need to amputate your foot."

"*What?* Oh my God! That's insane! No way! *No! No! No!*"

"Look Aaron, I said *very* worst-case, and I really don't see it coming to that. What we're going to do is just keep you here overnight and see what the situation looks like in the morning."

* * *

Dr. Levine had someone call Vicki at work and tell her that her husband was in the hospital and that she could stop by whenever she got off work.

When she got the call, Vicki came right over to the hospital. "Aaron, what the hell is going on? Last I knew, your foot was itching. How does that turn into you being in the hospital?"

Aaron tried to explain some of this to her, but it sounded weird even to him and way weirder to her. And the problem was that his foot was starting to hurt again and he needed the nurse to give him another shot of morphine which was going to mean he couldn't explain anything at all. So he told her to go home and they would call her in the morning when they had things figured out. When she left, she told him she was going back to her office to catch up on the work she had missed.

* * *

Next morning, the head nurse had Aaron brought down to do another set of X-rays. She told him Dr. Levine and Dr. Hoffmeyer would arrive to see him around lunchtime.

Aaron couldn't tell if he was going crazy or what. None of any of this made any sense to him. None of it made any sense to Vicki. And the fact of the matter was that Vicki's intense work schedule had left things strained between them lately anyway and this was not helping at all. He was glad they had called and told her to just go to work and they would let her know when there was more information.

Aaron had no idea what his foot looked like this morning. They left it loosely wrapped in some hospital gauze when they took him down for X-rays and he had no intention of taking a peek before the doctors arrived.

Dr. Levine and Dr. Hoffmeyer arrived about 12:30. Dr. Hoffmeyer began by telling Aaron that he had gone to the office where Aaron worked to see if he could find out anything more about the apple he had eaten, but no one there seemed to know anything about it. And no one else had reported any kind of issues related to apple trees sprouting from their skin. One woman had been out sick for a couple of days, but it was probably just a summer cold.

Then Dr. Levine said, "Aaron, let's see what's going on with your foot this morning." He took a pair of scissors and cut open the gauze. When Aaron—very reluctantly—looked down, he saw that the shoot had grown back again, and in fact seemed substantially bigger than before.

Dr. Levine sighed. "Aaron, I'm afraid it's considerably worse than any of us expected. As you can see, cutting the top off didn't kill it, it just pruned it temporarily. And unfortunately, the roots have been growing very fast as well. I've been looking at this morning's X-rays and I talked them over with the head surgeon here at the hospital. Yesterday, I told you it might be impossible to remove the roots from your foot surgically. I suggested it might be necessary to consider amputating your foot to prevent spreading some sort of infection throughout your body. This morning's X-rays, however, show us that in addition to its being effectively impossible to remove the roots from your foot, they have already started spreading to other parts of your body. We can see at least one root that has grown up your left leg and is now making its way down your right leg towards your right foot. In addition, that same root has also been branching out in a variety of directions throughout your body. If this were cancer, I would say it has metastasized. I don't know what to call anything in this situation."

"We discussed the possibility of trying to use radiation to kill it, but our suspicion is that the amount of radiation it would take would kill you first, and who knows what kind of mutations a dose of heavy radiation would induce in whatever the hell it is that's growing in you." Dr. Levine just sat there, looking drained.

Wait a minute, goddammit, Aaron thought. I came here with a damn pain in my foot. I came here to get it *fixed*. This is *not* real. This *cannot* be happening. Even as he was thinking all this, however, he could see the green shoot from his foot growing visibly. When Dr. Levine first cut the bandages off, there were two leaves growing from it; now two more had sprouted.

Dr. Levine spoke up again: "I've put out a call to the other hospitals around the city and top hospitals around the country to see if anyone has had any experience like this. One of the teaching hospitals we contacted said they had no idea, but they were sending it out to other major hospitals around the world. In the meantime, we could try putting you on chemo, but as you may know that's very unpleasant, and we have no idea if it would do any good at all. For all we know, chemo might be a kind of high-powered plant food for this thing."

* * *

It was late evening when Vicki came to see him again. She was not at all happy to be there. "This *cannot* be happening. This cannot be happening *now!* You don't *understand.* I have a *huge* fucking presentation to finish for a major new client, and the truth is my fucking *job* is on the line. This is my *career,* goddammit! And no, you didn't know that. But the bottom line is, I just don't have fucking time for this."

"Look Aaron, I'm sorry about all this. Really, I am. Maybe I loved you, maybe we loved each other, who knows anymore? But the truth is, whatever this is, it is just too fucking weird for me to handle. And I *can't* handle it. I am *not* going to sit around trying to figure out ways to *deal* with something that *should not* be happening. I'm sorry I won't be there for you, but the truth is I won't be."

As she turned and walked out of the room, was she crying? It was hard to tell. It probably didn't matter anyway. Not much mattered anymore.

* * *

The next morning, Aaron felt the toes of his left foot getting very cold. When he looked, his toes were blue, even while the plant sprouting from the middle of his foot looked greener and more verdant than ever.

When Dr. Levine stopped in to see him, Aaron asked him about his toes. Dr. Levine looked much less surprised than Aaron would have thought. "I had told you about the root system growing in your foot. It looks as if the roots are cutting off the circulation to your toes to maximize the amount of oxygen and nutrients that they can feed to the plant itself. Your toes are of no use to the plant. I'm sorry."

* * *

They moved Aaron to the rehab section. It wasn't that they could do much for him by way of rehabilitation, but they couldn't do much for him medically either, and at least this unit had some lounges and open areas where patients could simply relax.

* * *

His first morning in his new room, Aaron felt something different about the soles of his feet. It was as if he had spaghetti moving around down there. He realized this was just another step being taken by the root system. It was ready to outgrow its pot.

Aaron, however, was not ready to, so to speak, put down roots just yet. He had the nurse bring him a big roll of tinfoil, folded some sheets four layers thick, and wrapped them around the bottoms of his feet to keep the roots from being able to break through to the ground, to the carpet, or anything at all.

But no matter what he did, he couldn't stop what was happening. He could see new shoots beginning to break through on his arms and on his legs. He could feel some pain in his left ear, as though something was trying to break through his eardrum in search of sunlight. And he knew all too well that his brain was just another source of nutrients in this inevitable process.

And even though he knew that it would only help fuel the plant's growth, he wanted to be able to lie back in the hospital's solarium and just feel the warm sun on his body. He couldn't stop what was happening, and by now it didn't even seem to hurt anymore.

* * *

"Why me?" Aaron asked. "Why me?"

He had asked Dr. Levine, and Dr. Levine just sat there. "Why *you*?" he said. "Why anyone? Why *not* you? That's the question that being a doctor doesn't give me answers to. I love helping people. But I can't help you, and that's driving me crazy. Why *you*? Why *me*? Why did *you* have to be *my* patient?"

Aaron would've asked Vicki. But Vicki had no interest. Aaron had become some weird kind of freak. And, in terms of *her* life, he was now an inconvenience she had no time for.

Could he have asked his friends? No one had come to visit him. He hadn't told anyone else about where he was and what was happening to him. And if they saw him in this condition, what would be the good?

Aaron wondered if a rabbi or some other religious person would have an answer. But what could they tell him about a God who would decide that this should happen to him?

He had wept when he first grasped the reality of his situation and his own futility in the face of it. As the days went on, he faded in and out of frustration and rage and found himself falling into indifference. The only future for him now was the green shoots sprouting from all over his body.

* * *

It was midafternoon. Aaron was lying half-asleep in the sun on a lounge chair in the solarium. A woman in a white nurse's uniform walked in. She was young-ish, mid-20s, maybe 30, dark hair, blue eyes. A tat-tooed garland of vines and brightly colored flowers grew up from her left ankle and wound its way up her left leg until it disappeared under the hem of her dress.

"I'm Eva," she said. "I heard about you and I wanted to see you. I know there was a doctor here who had tried to find out about the apples you had eaten. But the morning he went to your office, the woman who had brought the apples was away. I went by in the afternoon and she had come back and I asked her about the apples. She had bought them from an old lady at a farmers' market a couple of blocks from your office. The woman was dressed all in black and she had all these apples which she was selling at half the price of anybody else's apples. She said her apples grew so fast that she had to sell them cheap to get rid of them all. One of the farmers tried to dissuade the girl from buying them; he was saying something about them being 'devil apples.' But they were absolutely beautiful, absolutely bright red and glowing in the sunlight.

"The girl had bought a bag full and brought them back to the office. She had one left when I got there and she gave it to me. I ate it on the spot, even with everything I already knew about it. It was the best ap-ple I ever tasted."

Eva could see the shoot growing out of Aaron's foot—it had already tripled in size, and you could almost see it grow. But there were also new sprouts, just popping out, on his hands and on his arms. They no longer caused him pain; they were simply part of who he was, this new being.

Eva looked at him again, and then leaned down and kissed him on the lips. Aaron felt her tongue push gently into his mouth. When she pulled away, she said, "You taste of fresh apple, you taste of apple trees and springtime and new growth. I can taste why this has happened to you. I can tell you are a very special person. I wish we could have sex together, it would be so beautiful. But it's too late, too late for that now."

She went on, "You know, I can feel it growing in me too. It's still very young and hasn't broken through anywhere yet, but it feels very beautiful to me. In a few days, maybe a week or so, when it has really taken hold and is ready, I will go over to Prospect Park and find the perfect spot. It will probably be somewhere along the trail where you used to jog. And I will take off my shoes and stand there barefoot, wearing only a thin cotton dress with no buttons or zippers or anything artificial. And I will stand there on the rich ground and let the roots take hold and I will enter into a new destiny. And I will be thinking of you. And when I am grown, and when I am covered with bright red apples, families will come with their children to pick my apples. And I will be fulfilled. Be happy."

As she walked out of the room, Aaron was drifting back into sleep.

* * *

At the moment Aaron finally died, there was no one else in the room. When the nurse came in a half hour later, she almost couldn't tell because of all of the green shoots sprouting up all over him. She had to call a doctor with a stethoscope to confirm that Aaron's heart was no longer beating.

* * *

When Aaron died, Vicki wasn't there. Too much work was part of it perhaps. But the big part was that the whole fucking thing was too fucking crazy and she just didn't want any part of it anymore. She was *done*.

Not quite done, actually. There was, as they say, just one more thing. Vicki wanted Aaron's body cremated. Burned totally to ashes. Nothing left. Especially not a single fucking leaf, root, or green sprout anywhere.

There was only one problem. When he had turned 30, Aaron had decided to get things in order, and one of the things he did was to set out a will which specified he was to be buried in a green cemetery—no embalming, no fancy caskets, nothing, just let his body go back to the earth. He had filed his final disposition wishes with Dr. Levine, and with the hospital administration, to make sure they were part of the official record.

Vicki might've tried to file some sort of a suit to override Aaron's final request, but it would've taken time, and how would she have explained it to a court anyway?

* * *

Aaron was buried at the Evergreen Natural Cemetery in north Brooklyn. It was relatively new, but there was a lot of demand, and it had been filling up quickly. The space they found for Aaron's body ended up being very near the center of the whole cemetery.

The funeral service was arranged by the Evergreen staff. It was an overcast day, with intermittent sprinkles of rain. The ceremony was attended by Dr. Levine and Dr. Hoffmeyer, along with a few members of the Brooklyn Running Club who had known Aaron. Aside from the funeral director, who read some passages about the mission of the green cemetery and the passage of life to life, no one had any idea of what to say.

Vicki was not there. Vicki was not even in Brooklyn. Or New York. She had talked to her boss and requested an *immediate* transfer to their office in Phoenix. "Good luck growing a fucking apple tree anywhere around here in *this* heat," she told herself.

Dr. Levine had gotten a call early that morning from a doctor at one of the major teaching hospitals in Manhattan. He wanted to arrange a conference call for that afternoon for Dr. Levine and Dr. Hoffmeyer, along with some doctors and specialists from two other area hospitals, and an official from the Center for Disease Control, who wanted to know if they needed to start taking steps on this issue. Dr. Levine sighed. It was going to be a very long day.

* * *

Sure enough, with the onset of summer the shoots from Aaron's body quickly began to push through the warm earth to the surface and joined together to become a magnificent apple tree. At the same time, the root system began to reach out in all directions, seeking other bodies for nourishment and opportunities for growth. With surprising speed, the cemetery converted from an open burial ground to a dense forest, luring visitors from all of Brooklyn and even the other boroughs with its magnificent crop of apples every fall.

* * *

In the years that followed, no news source ever identified the start of the invasion. Of course they could see the famous forest in north Brooklyn, but there were also the trees in Prospect Park and in Central Park, and then New Jersey and Connecticut, and then still more trees in an ever-increasing range, now seemingly without end.

* * *

Dr. Levine was an old man now. Dr. Hoffmeyer, with whom he had become friends, had died of a heart attack some years before. Dr. Levine had retired from his practice very early, and had moved to a senior living community in Florida. The highlight of the facility was a huge wooden porch looking out at the ocean. Dr. Levine could be seen sitting there in his white rocking chair wearing his faded blue bathrobe every day, staring out at the waves with a haunted look in his eyes, forever unable to forget, and forever unable to forgive himself.

RUDOLPH AT REST—
A CHRISTMAS STORY

IT WAS 11:00 A.M. when Rudolph finally came into the kitchen at the North Pole Retired Reindeer Home. As usual, the place was a mess. Dirty dishes left in the sink, empty bottles scattered pretty much everywhere. He reached down to pick up the newspaper from the floor where one of the other residents had dropped it. It was a clumsy process with his mechanical hands. The elves had made the hands for him as a gift, on their own time. They still remembered him and tried to help him and some of the other old-timer reindeer out.

They weren't the most professional prosthetic hands—they only had three fingers, or rather one thumb and two fingers—but they let him do a lot of basic things. Most importantly, they were good enough to let him hold on to a glass or a bottle.

He tried to smooth the paper out on the table so he could read it. Despite his famous nose, he had never been the brightest bulb in class and reading was still a challenge. And these days it was getting harder and harder to concentrate and stay focused. It was easier to just drink.

And frankly, the North Pole Retired Reindeer Home was a dump. It wasn't at the North Pole anyway, it was in a run-down section of northern Minneapolis.

* * *

It had been better when he first came to Minneapolis. The new management at the North Pole had given all the reindeer a very fine retirement dinner, and thanked them all for their many years of dedicated service. And when he got to Minneapolis, the Retired Reindeer Home he arrived at was a in very nice gothic-looking building that had originally been built by a local church to provide a comfortable home for their elderly parishioners. It had had lush green lawns and adjoining woods, and he and the other reindeer would spend their days hanging out, enjoying each other's company and reminiscing about the old days.

But that was then. Now, a lot of things had changed.

* * *

It all started when Santa died.

Actually, thinking back, there were signs before that. Santa had always been overweight of course—that was part of the package. Plus-size and jolly.

Age had never really appeared to make much of a difference for Santa. He seemed eternal. Rumor had it he was actually hundreds of years old, and we all pretty much expected him to live forever. Even the elves and the reindeer never seemed to age. Rudolph wasn't sure how old *he* was, but he was sure he had been around a lot longer than the 15 years or so he would have been expected to live in the regular world.

But somehow, that past year Santa had started becoming noticeably heavier. He had always been brisk and energetic in a very jolly sort of way. Now he was slower, and seemed to stay sitting a lot more. The Christmas deadline was still there, same as always, but everyone began to wonder if he was going to be able to pull it off.

Mrs. Claus was worried and began to urge Santa to watch his diet for his health's sake. She even wanted him to go see a cardiologist for a check-up. They had been married for a very long time and were always very loving and affectionate, but now Santa was becoming short-tempered and impatient with her— "That bitch. She's always nagging at me," he would tell the elves. And then he would eat more than ever. And drink more too.

It was not only Santa. The elves also seemed to be slowing down. They would take breaks instead of working non-stop, and some would even knock off early. They had always been cheerful and efficient, but now they would complain about the cold and the pain in their joints. Even Rudolph and the other reindeer seemed to be becoming creakier and more sensitive to the cold.

The toys were becoming a problem too. In the old days it was stuffed animals and dolls and wooden toys. Santa tried not to give children clothing—he knew they hated getting clothes instead of real presents. But now they all wanted this electronic crap—tablets and TVs and game stations. Santa's elves were out of their depth on this stuff and had to bring in hired elves from China and India to help out.

"Damn electronic junk! Damn kids!" Santa had been heard to mutter after a bit too much eggnog.

* * *

It hadn't been like that in the old days.

Growing up wasn't always easy for Rudolph. His nose was oversized and the other reindeer at school called him all sorts of names—"snot-nose," "wart hog," "clown face," "freak"—and basically treated him like shit.

As he got older and moved into adolescence, his nose changed from being big and warty-brown to dull red and then continued to get brighter and brighter.

None of this helped. Being a freak with a bright red nose wasn't something anyone, including Rudolph, saw as a big improvement.

When he and the other reindeer graduated and moved to Santa's stables, Santa was much nicer to him than the others had been. But he had no particular reason to see Rudolph as a member of his starting line-up.

Rudolph did get to participate in the regular physical training and workouts, and he was determined to get into as good shape as any of the others. But he knew none of that would make any difference.

And so it went, year after year. And then...

* * *

Yeah, you know the story. One foggy Christmas Eve and all that. Well, that's pretty much it. The elves had to do a rush job to fix up an additional harness for Rudolph at the head of the pack. And you should have heard the bitching from all the other reindeer.

Still, at the end of the night, they all had to acknowledge that they couldn't have done it without him. And so they warmed up to him, sort of.

Rudolph, however, wasn't ready to forgive and forget. He knew damn well what a bunch of bastards they all were.

But now, things were different. Very different. Suddenly Rudolph not only had Santa's praise, he was also a chick magnet. All the does were mooning over him. Even the cute young female elves used to come out and pet him and flirt with him. Not that anything ever happened on that score, of course, but it felt damn good to be the star for a change.

And so, Rudolph began doing what any right-thinking young male reindeer would do. Donner and Blitzen and Comet and all the rest, they had thought *they* were the rock stars. Now it was Rudolph who was banging every female reindeer in sight.

After that, Rudolph led the way every Christmas Eve. *He* was the star. And he thought it could go on forever...

* * *

Anyway, it was Rudolph's fifth Christmas when it happened. Maybe his sixth—it was hard to keep track of the years up there.

Every December, various mathematicians, physicists and engineers would write columns crunching the numbers and proving definitively Santa's around-the-world-in-one-night delivery feat was logically impossible. Santa's sleigh would burn to a crisp someplace in southern California. Or maybe Shanghai. Or wherever.

They just didn't get it. It wasn't logic or science that ruled where Santa was concerned. It just *happened*. Get over it.

This year, however, things were getting off to a rockier start. It was time to go and the elves were still not finished loading the toys onto the sleigh. And Santa was having a hard time just hoisting himself up into his seat.

The reindeer were getting antsy. Even under the best conditions, they were facing a trip of tens of thousands of miles, mostly at a full gallop, with millions of short stops—an endless cycle of house-to-house wind sprints. And here they were, losing essential time.

Finally, the elves managed to help push Santa into place and toss the last bags of toys onto the sleigh. As an extra precaution, one of the elves was added to sit beside Santa and help with the steering. They were ready to take off. There wasn't much fog to speak of, but they would definitely need Rudolph's extra help if they were to make it.

They headed out at full speed and were soon flying over homes of sleeping boys and girls. But almost immediately things began to go wrong. At the very first house, a now enormous Santa got stuck in the chimney and the elf had to pull with all his might to help get Santa out. After that, the elf had to take over chimney and delivery duties while Santa tried to sort out which toys went to each house.

It was very unprofessional, and pretty soon all of them, Santa, the elf, and the reindeer felt themselves losing the spirit of Christmas. Which only made things worse, since it was the spirit of Christmas that allowed them to do all this in a single night in the first place.

In the end, they did deliver all the presents to all the right homes. But the final deliveries, rather than being made at midnight or even in the general middle of the night, were squeaked in as dawn began to break and eager children were already beginning to wake up.

They still had a long run back to the North Pole. Along the way, Dasher, who had been breathing heavily for much of the trip, suddenly stopped moving. This threw the team out of balance and the elf was barely able to make a controlled landing in a heavily wooded area in northern Lapland. When the elf got out to see what was up, he found Dasher's body was already growing cold and stiff. His heart had given out sometime after leaving the last house. Dasher's body was much too heavy for Santa and the elf to lift onto the back of the sleigh to bring home. So very sadly and reluctantly they had to leave him propped up against a tree there in the snow.

They moved Rudolph into Dasher's space to balance out the team, and unhooked Rudolph's lead harness. Then they took off for a final and very somber trip home.

By the time they got back, it was clear that Santa was not well. His normally rosy cheeks had gone pale and he was shivering. They tried to help him inside, but just as he got down from the sleigh, he suddenly clutched his chest and pitched forward into the snow.

The other elves had come out to greet Santa on his return. Now they rushed to help. They dragged him inside and tried CPR for nearly half an hour. It was no use. Santa was dead.

Mrs. Claus was hysterical. "I told him to take care of himself. I warned him over and over, didn't I? But did he listen to me? Of course not."

The elves didn't know what to say to her, or to each other, as they waited for the doctor to arrive.

*   *   *

After that, of course, everything changed. Everyone knew Santa's work must go on. But how?

Until now, no one had worried about anything. Money. Organization. Supplies. It all just seemed to *happen*.

Now...what?

* * *

They had never announced Santa's death to the world. The funeral was small and very private—Mrs. Claus, the elves and the reindeer. Santa was buried in an open, snow-covered field behind the workshop. No one was even supposed to know.

A few days later, however, they heard a strange sound in the distance. It was a helicopter. Inside was Kris Svensen, the toy tycoon.

Kris liked to describe himself as a "grown-up kid," and he had always regarded Santa as the patron saint in his life. He had found out—never mind how— about the situation, and realized it was his destiny to carry on Santa's work for the generations of children to come.

Kris knew toys—he had toy stores in countries around the world—and he knew how to handle challenges with tight deadlines. He was ready. And he had a trusted team of people to help him with all the planning details.

* * *

The very next week, Kris held a meeting with the reindeer from Santa's team. He appreciated the very loyal service they had given over the years, he explained, but he also knew the toll recent events had taken on them. He was offering them an opportunity to retire, and he was establishing a new North Pole Retired Reindeer Home where they could live rent-free as long as they wanted. He had already found the perfect building on the grounds of a church in Minneapolis. In addition to their pensions, they would receive a generous severance payment that would allow them to enjoy some degree of luxury in their lives.

The reindeer agreed to his proposal, partly because they didn't seem to have much choice. But also, that last ride and Santa's death *had* taken a toll on them. No matter what, things wouldn't be the same.

* * *

It was good at first at the retirement home. It was clean and comfortable and the food was excellent. The staff was always eager to find fun things for them to do. In Rudolph's case, the social worker suggested he might enjoy the chance to pull a sleigh at children's parties during the rest of the winter. Rudolph agreed, and they set him up with a whole series of parties and events all over the country. He loved being around the children and they loved meeting the famous Rudolph whom they had all heard about.

It was fun going to all those parties and being around all those happy children, but when the winter season was over and the snow was all gone, he realized he didn't have anything else to do. He decided to head back to Minneapolis.

* * *

When Rudolph got back, he discovered that the North Pole Retired Reindeer Home had moved. The original building had been very nice of course, but it had also been very expensive. As the new accountants had quickly noticed, there were plenty of lower-cost options available.

The new location was in a former one-story apartment building in a slightly run-down industrial area on the north side of Minneapolis. The building had been in foreclosure, and what with new city regulations requiring owners to maintain their properties at their own expense, the bank was happy to sell it for practically nothing.

The staff from the original Retired Reindeer Home hadn't been invited to stay on at the new location. Instead, services were being handled by a management company, which could be contacted by phone during office hours.

Rudolph was discouraged by what he found. So were the other reindeer. Blitzen and Rudolph had become friends after they had been ushered into retirement—they were all in this together now, regardless of past differences.

Blitzen told Rudolph some of the elves had stopped by for a visit while he was away. The new management at the North Pole had determined that most of the elves could be let go to be replaced by new hires who were younger and worked for a lot less money. And increasingly, toy production was being outsourced to elf factories in countries like Indonesia, Thailand and Bangladesh.

As for the old elves, they too had been offered a retirement home, only theirs would be in Florida. Many of the elves were tired of being cold, and for them, unlike the reindeer, the idea of hot weather sounded fine. They had been rather pleased when the arrangement was first mentioned, but seeing the condition of the Reindeer Home, they were sounding a lot less certain.

"What about Santa?" Rudolph asked.

"Well," Blitzen said, "it's actually going to be Santa*S* now. Even the logistics consultant they brought in from some big-name firm couldn't figure out how Santa had been covering the whole world in that time frame."

"He was *Santa*, dammit!" Rudolph exclaimed. "Of course they can't figure it out."

"Well, it seems like they're going to split it up— maybe have a dozen or so Santas. But that's going to cost a lot, even if they go cut-rate. They were talking about maybe having to red-line some areas to make it work."

"And what about the reindeer? And the flying? You know none of us could fly without Santa."

"Well, they're trying to get some reindeer from Russia on the cheap. I guess they think they'll figure something out. Me, I think that's bullshit. We were the only ones."

The whole thing was just a bummer.

* * *

Increasingly, Rudolph found himself thinking about the old days, and about what had happened to some of the other reindeer.

Cupid had decided to come out as transgendered. He figured he could make some money (no, not a quick buck) on the talk show circuit. He was fine in New York, San Francisco, L.A., even Austin. But then he decided to appear on some talk shows in the Deep South. The other reindeer had warned him... Hell, begged him not to go. Of course he wouldn't listen. And sure enough, his first day in Alabama he got run down by a couple of rednecks in a bright red pickup truck with a big Confederate flag decal all across the back window. Some people who happened to see it said the guys in the truck were yelling, "Ye haw! Got that queer!"

Cupid was lying there in agony and a local cop had to administer the final coup de grâce with his pistol. He thought Cupid was just an ordinary deer. When he was told this had been one of Santa's reindeer, he felt really shook up about it, didn't want his kids to hear about it at all. Still, he said, "warn't much else I coulda done nohow."

Rudolph wasn't quite sure about that line of reasoning. Is that what the cop would have done to a fellow officer wounded in a shoot-out? Officer down. Bang.

But Rudolph knew he couldn't change any of that. Hell. Most all of the old gang was gone by now.

Prancer had died of AIDS. They had put him on retrovirals, but he kept forgetting to take them. It was some weird form of denial. "What kind of Santa's reindeer goes around taking retrovirals?" he would say.

Vixen, who had always been one of Rudolph's favorites, had met some caribou from Canada and they had headed out to Maine to stake out some territory.

None of it was good. He and Blitzen had lost touch with most of the others.

As the days went on, the two of them spent less time talking and more time drinking. Sometimes Rudolph would pass out before he could make it back to his room.

* * *

Summer was long and hot and he spent most of his time indoors with the shades drawn.

In the fall, however, things cooled down, and by the beginning of November they had their first snowfall. The cold weather lifted Rudolph's spirits, but when he thought about Christmas without Santa, without the elves, without the other reindeer, he grew morose again.

Then, one day in mid-December, a group of children came to the Home to sing Christmas carols for the reindeer. The children were very sweet and eager to bring joy. All was going well until they started singing, "Rudolph the Red-Nosed Reindeer." They didn't know. Rudolph's nose had long ago lost its glow, and it was no more red than all the other reindeer who drank too much.

As the children sang, Rudolph's eyes began to tear up, and by the end he was crying very hard but trying to keep it from showing. When they left, however, his crying turned into deep sobbing. He sobbed for Santa, for the elves, for all the reindeer including himself. He sobbed for everything that had been lost.

* * *

It was hard to sleep that night. Rudolph's dreams were one tragedy after another.

During the night it began to snow and by morning the falling snow was so thick you could hardly see across the street.

Rudolph got up early. He couldn't stand trying to sleep anymore. When he looked out, his heart leaped. He had missed this so much.

Suddenly he knew what he had to do. He had to go home—his real home, at the North Pole. He had never even gone back to visit Santa's grave. Now it was time.

He knew north. That was easy. It would be a long way, but that didn't matter. Time didn't matter anymore.

He felt younger and freer than he had in years. He pulled off the prosthetic hands and left them. He began walking, then galloping, then walking again. After an hour or so, he found himself at the side of a huge highway. It was Interstate 694 on the north edge of Minneapolis.

He looked. How many lanes was it? Six lanes each way? Eight? Ten?

Despite the blinding snow, traffic was heavy. The big trucks didn't have the option of taking the day off, no matter how bad the weather.

Rudolph watched carefully, trying to judge their speed and see when there might be a gap. He wasn't used to this and it was confusing to try to figure out. But the North Pole was on the other side, and he had no choice.

Rudolph looked again, both ways. "I'm coming Santa. I'm coming home," he said softly to himself.

And then he leaped out onto the highway.

MEINE YIDDISCHE BARBIE

BARBIE (NOT YET "SHEILA" OF COURSE) came into Esther's life as a present for her 11th birthday.

Esther's father, Leo, was a partner in a small law firm in Brooklyn. He was widely respected for his legal expertise, and even more importantly, he was known to be a real mensch in all his dealings with his clients. It happened that Leo had done a pro bono job helping an elderly woman save her home from foreclosure. She was deeply grateful, as were all the members of her family. One of her nephews was an actor who had played minor roles in a few popular sitcoms, but had started out doing magic shows and still enjoyed doing magic for audiences of young people. He was happy to do a show for Leo for free, as a mitzvah to show his gratitude.

The actor's name, or more accurately the names of the sitcoms he had appeared in, was sure to make this party a big deal among Esther's friends. And so, Esther's father decided to make Esther's birthday party an occasion for her to invite more people than her usual circle of friends to celebrate.

The party was held in the backyard, which was barely large enough to hold everyone. The magic show was a great success, and lots of the kids lined up afterwards to get the actor's autograph. Needless to say, Esther ended up with way more birthday presents than she'd ever gotten before.

One of the presents was a classic Barbie doll. It was given to her by a girl named Taffy, who was a very nice girl, but most decidedly not Jewish.

When the party was over and the guests had left, Esther and her parents carried the presents back into the house and put them down in the living room.

Esther's father was delighted with how well everything had gone. Esther's mother, Ada, was happy as well, but as was her nature, she couldn't help worrying about all sorts of little things.

* * *

Now at last, Esther had a chance to look at her pile of presents. One present stood out among all the rest—the golden-haired Barbie doll. Esther knew Barbies existed, but she had never seen one up close. She took it out of the box and looked at it.

Esther's father was still basking in the satisfaction of a wonderful party. But now, Esther's mother's attention fixed on what Esther was holding in her hand.

Esther's mother took one look at Barbie with the pink miniskirt, with the blonde hair, blue eyes and *goyishe* upturned nose, and a look of alarm spread over her face. "Esther. Esther, do you see this? What *is* this? And this outfit? *Oy.* This is a *shiksa* doll. This is *not* a Jewish doll. This is *not* a doll for a nice Jewish girl. Especially not for a nice Jewish girl who is getting ready to study for her bat mitzvah."

Esther looked stricken. She was so excited about her exotic new present. And now her mother was going to take it away?

"Esther, I know your friend, Taffy is it? Like the candy they sell at Coney Island? I know she meant well, but they're different. Different people. Of course you can be polite and thank her for the gift, but...well, I would just rather you have a Jewish doll instead."

Esther looked at her mother. It had been such a wonderful party, and she had been so happy, and this is how it would end? She felt almost as if she would burst into tears. "Mama, let me keep her. I can change her. You'll see. Maybe she can study Torah with me."

* * *

Barbie found herself feeling an unaccustomed level of doubt. Up until now, she was sure she was doing everything right. And her pink miniskirt, white sweater and pink jacket—that was the most popular Barbie outfit of all. Every Barbie wanted the pink miniskirt outfit. It had a little bit of that Jackie Kennedy glamour, and it was an outfit that was suitable for all occasions, from shopping at the mall to having tea with her friends. The idea that her outfit was not suitable... That her hair... How was she supposed to deal with that?

All the Barbies were anxious about their new owners. She had heard stories that circulated among the Barbies about the world out there. Lots of Barbies ended up with little girls who loved them and played with them every day; some of them had lots of other Barbies as well and they and their friends spent time dressing the Barbies in their favorite outfits and had them hold Barbie parties, and Barbie outings. Of course, there were also darker stories, about other girls and particularly about the brothers of these girls who sometimes—at least so it was whispered—were not very nice at all.

At least this Esther girl seemed very nice, but this was a situation she had never heard of and had no idea what she should do. Jewish she had heard of, and quite possibly there were some Jewish Barbies, but she had never met any of them.

Barbie had been overhearing Esther's parents' conversation all during the party. They were Jewish, and being Jewish was important to them. They tried to take Esther to Temple at least one or two Saturdays a month, and on Passover, Esther's mother and her two aunts would take turns hosting a big family Seder for all the relatives. And now, of course, they were looking forward to Esther's bat mitzvah, which would signify Esther's own entrance into the world of Jewish tradition. Where did Barbie fit in in all this? It was simple. She didn't. She was an outcast—a blonde-haired, blue-eyed, pink mini-skirted outcast.

* * *

Already this argument between Esther and her mother had undermined what had been on course to be the best birthday of Esther's life.

At least her mother hadn't forbidden her outright to keep her Barbie. But Esther knew she had to do something, something that would get this Barbie into her mother's good graces.

Esther took the Barbie up to her room and thought hard.

First, she decided to give her her own name— Sheila Barbie. Esther knew that "Barbie" had to be part of the name, but thought maybe it could be a last name, since there were so many of them.

"Sheila Barbie" sounded good, it sounded just right. Esther was feeling better already.

Then Esther went online to Etsy to see what she could find that might help. She found a shop called, "Jewish Stuff for Jewish Girls." The woman who created the shop had a write-up in which she discussed the Barbie doll she had loved when she was a young girl. Her Barbie had had the same problem—blonde hair, miniskirt, not Jewish at all. She loved her Barbie, but she always felt conflicted. So, when she got married and had a daughter, she wanted to let her daughter have a conflict-free Barbie. And now she was offering the same things she had come up with for her daughter to other young Jewish girls facing the same situation.

Esther was delighted. Because of the turnout at her birthday party, she had quite a bit of birthday *gelt*, and even though the prices were high, she felt sure she could afford pretty much whatever it would take.

Esther knew Sheila Barbie's blonde hair was a major issue. But here at the Jewish Stuff shop, she could buy Barbie a beautiful black-haired wig—made from real human hair (from long-haired Jewish girls in Eastern Europe who were happy to make some extra money just by growing their hair). This hair would not only be black, it would be *real*, way better than Barbie's original blonde hair made from who knows what.

Plus, Esther found the perfect outfit. She had to have her father order it online using his credit card, but since she had the money to pay him up front, he was happy to help her out—and to keep it quiet from her mother until it arrived.

It took the package two weeks to arrive; the outfit had to be custom sewn by hand. Fortunately, they had had one last black-haired wig in stock, or the wait would've been much longer.

* * *

The package was waiting for Esther when she got home from school in the afternoon. She saw her mother was curious, but wasn't asking any questions for now.

Esther almost ran up the stairs to her room with the package. When she unwrapped it, there everything was.

She started by putting the new wig over Barbie's original blonde hair. It fit perfectly, and the transformation was immediate. With her luxurious dark hair, Barbie immediately became 90 percent less *shiksa*. The pink miniskirt, however, certainly did not reflect anything about Jewish culture or tradition as Esther knew it.

Besides the wig, Esther had ordered different underwear, and a charcoal gray wool skirt, with a matching jacket with black velvet trim. The skirt reached down below Barbie's knees, about halfway down her calf, and the jacket buttoned up to the neck.

Esther took off the outfit Barbie was wearing, including the stylish bra and tiny panties. Then she began by putting on conservative, thick white cotton underwear. After that, she put on the gray wool jacket and skirt.

Esther then took off Barbie's high-heeled sandals. She put on dark stockings to cover her legs, and replaced the sandals with sensible black lace-up shoes, with only the slightest hint of the heel being at all higher.

This was not precisely the kind of outfit Esther herself would wear; it was the kind of outfit that the most conservative reaches of her mind said she probably should wear, at least some of the time. In any case, it changed pretty much everything about Barbie. Now she really did look like Sheila Barbie.

Esther was delighted. But, as she kept looking at Sheila Barbie, she still wasn't seeing herself, even beyond Barbie's often maligned proportions. No, even with the hair and the clothes, Sheila Barbie's intense blue eyes still gave her away.

Esther went back to the Jewish Stuff website. Sure enough, they had also come up with a solution to this problem. They sold a pack of two dark brown eye stickers to be applied over the original blue. It was four dollars for the two-pack, plus shipping. She had her dad order it as soon as he got home.

This time, this package arrived in only four days. When Esther got home and found the package, she ran up to her room to apply the finishing touches.

The eye stickers fit perfectly, and looked perfect as well. There she was—Sheila, Meine Yiddishe Barbie.

* * *

All of this was strange to Barbie. She wasn't at all sure what to think. But then, when the eye stickers had been applied, and her hair and her outfit were all in place, Esther held her up to the mirror and Sheila Barbie could see her new self for the first time.

Barbie looked at this stranger looking back at her. But slowly, she began to realize she liked how this stranger looked. However attention-getting she had looked with her blonde hair and pink miniskirt, she had always felt slightly shallow, like someone who was never going to be taken very seriously.

Sheila Barbie was someone to be taken seriously.

* * *

When Esther showed her mother the new and im-proved Sheila Barbie, her mother was impressed and delighted. "What a *shana maidel*," she declared. "A beautiful Jewish doll for my beautiful Jewish daugh-ter."

And with that, Sheila Barbie was accepted.

* * *

For the new Sheila Barbie, there was much to learn.

Sometimes, when Barbie heard Esther's mother talking on the phone, or talking with some of her family members who had stopped by, Barbie couldn't understand a word. *Kishkas, tuchas, chutzpah, schmuck, dreck, bupkis.* All these strange words just flying about. Once in a while there would be a word dropped in that she could catch, but beyond that, it was as if the mother was speaking some strange private language, guttural and foreign.

She noticed that even Esther did not entirely understand these conversations, although Esther's vocabulary included a lot of words Barbie had never heard before and struggled to try to figure out.

One word Sheila Barbie did learn and loved was "*nu.*" It filled in for just about any situation. Any time she wasn't quite sure what was going on, she would think to herself "*nu?*"

* * *

Esther had been going to shul for several years already, and had been learning to read and write Hebrew. But now, with only a year to go until her bat mitzvah, it was time to get really focused.

Several afternoons a week, Esther would come home from school and go up to her room to study her Torah lessons. Esther would set Sheila Barbie on the desk while she was studying, so that Sheila Barbie could look on while she recited.

*"Barukh atah Adonai Eloheinu melekh
ha-olam shehakol bara lichvodo. —*

*Blessed are You, LORD, our G-d, sover-
eign of the universe, who created everything for His Glory."*

Sheila Barbie loved the sounds and the rhythm of
the prayers and the Torah texts, and she worked hard
to memorize as much as she possibly could. When Esther was off at school, or any other time Sheila Barbie
was left on her own, she would take the opportunity
to try to recite as much as she could from memory.

It was hard work, but it didn't feel like work at all
to Sheila Barbie. It was so exciting and so challenging.
As an ordinary Barbie, no one would have ever
thought to challenge her to learn anything at all. As it
was, Sheila Barbie was such a fast learner that soon
she began to feel she knew the lessons better than Esther. When Esther would hesitate, or falter, Sheila
Barbie wished she could speak up and help prompt
her memory.

When Esther finally had her bat mitzvah, she
made sure to bring Sheila Barbie along in her big bag,
so that Sheila Barbie could hear everything for herself.
Esther had studied long and hard, and at the ceremony, she did an exceptional job. The rabbi congratulated her, her parents congratulated her, and all her
friends congratulated her. Sheila Barbie would've congratulated her as well if she had a chance, but in all
honesty, she also felt she herself deserved at least a
little bit of the credit.

* * *

Outside of Torah studies, Sheila Barbie loved Esther's family's parties and get-togethers.

What a torrent of conversation, of kvetching, of noodging, of angsting! They loved to schmooze. There were no awkward moments of silence, not even a second of silence. They talked about everything, including of course, politics. They were all Jews, they were all family—but *oy*, when it came to politics... voices got loud, and tempers got heated. Esther's mother regularly had to step in and remind everybody that politics were off-limits: *"Genug ist genug!"* Unfortunately, there were very few topics that people did not end up arguing about, so Esther's mother was constantly bringing in fresh trays of snacks to distract everyone.

Sheila Barbie loved it all. The talk, the energy, the arguments. With the other Barbies, she had never argued at all. And back then, who knew from politics?

How Sheila Barbie wished she could schmooze like that. It had such weight, such energy, it seemed so fascinating. From her days of talking with the other Barbies, she could not remember a single thing that any of them had said. But here, she was rapt. She wanted to remember every word, she wanted to learn it all. She was bursting with the enormousness of everything.

* * *

As Esther grew older and entered high school, she spent less and less time playing with Sheila Barbie, although she would still sometimes talk to her about things that were on her mind and ask her what she thought. Most of the time however, Sheila Barbie just sat there on the top of the dresser as a quiet reminder of Esther's best aspirations.

The summer after her sophomore year in high school, Esther took a trip out to Coney Island with four of her friends—two boys and two other girls, all Jewish. "Don't eat the hotdogs," her mother implored her, "not even if they dare you. From what they put in their hot dogs it's better none of us should know. But don't, please, please don't eat them."

That night, after Ester had gotten home and was getting ready for bed, she sat down with Sheila Barbie. "I did something today, Sheila Barbie," she whispered. "I... tried a hot dog. We all did—we bought one foot-long and each of us took a bite." Ester looked to see Barbie's reaction. "You see, we just wanted to know. What it was like. Why it was such a big deal. And it was pretty good. I guess if I wasn't Jewish, I would eat them a lot." She paused. "But," she added after another minute, "it's not so bad. This way I have momma's matzah balls, and kugel, and lots of stuff I love and the *goyim* don't have. I don't know, though, I might be willing to give up playing dreidel in exchange for being able to eat hot dogs."

* * *

Esther was a bright girl, and studied hard and got excellent grades in all her subjects. When it came time for college, she could pick and choose from among the best. And what she chose was New York University. NYU was an outstanding school, with a reputation that kept getting better and better. Esther loved the idea of the excitement of the city, and her parents were pleased she would be only a subway ride away for her to see them.

Esther got a suite with three other girls in a new dormitory building. It wasn't cheap, but it was new and clean and had lots of security features, which was what mattered most to all their parents. The suite had a central living room/TV room for the girls to hang out in, and each girl had a very small bedroom of their own, with a bed, a tiny closet, a chest of drawers, and a small desk for studying. Esther set Sheila Barbie on the chest of drawers where she could keep Esther company when she was studying or just lounging around.

In the beginning, everything was going well. Esther was excited about her new courses, and even though the work was hard, she never complained. She studied most nights, and on the weekends would sometimes go out with one or more of her roommates to look around, and to get something to eat at a nearby restaurant. Esther talked to her parents a couple times a week on the phone, but she was so busy with her coursework that she didn't get back out to Brooklyn until Thanksgiving, and then not again until winter break.

Sheila Barbie was very happy with this new chapter in her and Esther's life. From where she sat on the bureau, she could look out the window and get a bit of the view of the street below and see all the students going back and forth. What was most satisfying was watching Esther study and learn and grow. Sheila Barbie only wished she could be a student too, with all that hard and interesting work to do.

* * *

During the fall, the weather had stayed warmer longer than usual, and it seemed as if winter might be nothing more than a minor nuisance. When Esther got back to campus after break, however, winter began to make up for lost time. It was cold, it was dark, it was gloomy. Esther got her books for her new courses, and tried to settle in. But the weather was so depressing that it was hard for her to feel excited or pay as much attention as she should.

Esther seemed quieter and more withdrawn these days. Sheila Barbie could tell Esther was falling behind in her work, and that her heart just wasn't in it in the way it had been in the fall. Sometimes Esther would glance over at Sheila Barbie, but she didn't say anything. She just sat there, looking sad and depressed. She also started spending more time hanging out in the living room with her other roommates, watching TV, ordering in pizza, and, with increasing frequency, drinking wine and beer with them. During the fall, while the other girls were watching TV and hanging out, Esther had been the diligent one. But now that had changed.

Sheila Barbie was very upset. She wanted to help, to talk to Esther and encourage her and remind her what a terrific student she could be when she tried. But Esther barely glanced at her these days; when she did happen to look over at Sheila Barbie, it seemed somehow to make her uncomfortable.

* * *

Gradually, the weather began to turn, and if spring had not yet fully arrived, it was in the air. And of course, come spring, young girls' thoughts turn to... boys.

Although this dorm was supposed to be focused on providing a studious and academic environment, the evening TV watching, eating pizza and drinking beer quickly became a coed event, often with more boys than girls. Esther sometimes left her door ajar and Barbie could see the goings-on. These boys, she scowled. Not a yarmulke on any of them. Loud. *No-good-niks. Gonifs. Dreck.* These were not the sorts of boys Esther should be talking to at all. No. Sheila Barbie was adamant.

Sometimes Sheila Barbie would see one girl or another sitting on one of the sofas in the living room making out with some boy. What? What about the rules? There *must* be rules! Sheila Barbie didn't know any of the details about the rules, but she knew this was *not* right. Once she even spotted Esther making out with a boy on one of the sofas. The two of them would stop and laugh and giggle, and then go back to making out some more.

* * *

About a week later, Esther came into the bedroom one evening with the boy she had been making out with the other day. The boy looked over at Sheila Barbie and said to Esther, "What is *that*? Is that a *Barbie*? It doesn't look like any Barbie I've ever seen. Looks more like some kind of Debbie Downer to me."

Esther looked over at Sheila Barbie. She looked embarrassed for herself, for Sheila Barbie, and for the whole situation. She walked over and took Sheila Barbie and put her in the top dresser drawer along with her underwear and socks.

Sheila Barbie was shocked at what had just happened. In a drawer? Was *this* her new home? She lay there, in a jumble of underwear and some thick winter socks.

Meanwhile, Esther and the boy had gotten back to whatever they were doing, which seemed to include a lot of giggling and an occasional halfhearted, "We shouldn't," from Esther.

Sheila Barbie frowned. Hidden in the drawer, she couldn't see anything, she could only hear. And after a while what she was hearing was deeply disturbing.

"Are they *shtupping*?" She couldn't believe she was even thinking such a thing. But what other way was she to understand the grunting, the moaning, the sounds of the bed springs? She wanted to cover her ears, but of course she couldn't. "*No. No. No. No!*" Sheila Barbie wanted to scream. She was helpless. She felt utterly mortified this should be happening, and that she should have to bear her own kind of witness to it.

Eventually, the noises died down and finally stopped. Sheila Barbie listened. Even if it was over for them, she knew it would never be over for her.

All too soon however, was it two minutes, five minutes, who could tell? But sure enough, the same noises started up all over again. Shelia Barbie wished they could just burn her at the stake and get it over with. This, *this*, was unbearable.

* * *

For several days, nothing happened. Sheila Barbie lay there helpless in the drawer, and only occasionally would she hear the sounds of Esther puttering around in the bedroom.

Finally, she heard footsteps walking towards the chest of drawers. The drawer was pulled open, and Esther lifted out Sheila Barbie from where she had been hidden away. "Sheila Barbie, you know I love you, but I've been changing, and it's time for you to change too."

With that, Esther began removing Sheila Barbie's shoes, her gray jacket, her long skirt, and her heavy shapeless underwear. Sheila Barbie was mortified at being undressed this way, and of just lying there naked. Esther got out the box Barbie had come in on her birthday and got out Barbie's original clothes. She put on Barbie's Victoria's-Secret-style bra and bikini panties. Then she put on Barbie's pink miniskirt and a tightfitting, sleeveless white sweater. Then she added Barbie's original ankle strap high heels.

Esther looked at Barbie. Then she reached and pulled off Barbie's black wig, and let Barbie's long golden hair show once more. Then finally, she reached over and pulled the dark brown stickers from Barbie's bright blue eyes.

There she was, in all her original *shiksa* glory. Esther held Sheila Barbie up to the mirror so she could see for herself. Sheila Barbie looked, and was horrified. All that time, all that study, all that newfound seriousness and sense of purpose, all she had learned, and now this?

Esther had been hiding her in a drawer for the past week because of how she looked. Now it was Sheila Barbie's turn to want to hide in a drawer.

Esther put Sheila Barbie back on top of her bureau. Sheila Barbie said nothing.

* * *

It was late in the evening when Sheila Barbie saw the bedroom door open and Esther come in, giggling in a slightly tipsy way. She was holding the hand of a boy whom she was dragging along with her.

She closed the door behind them. The only light in the room was from the streetlights and other city lights outside. It didn't really matter. They were already pulling each other's clothes off, and as fast as they could manage, they were in bed together. It was just like the other night, although Sheila Barbie had no way to tell whether it was the same boy or a different one. And sure enough, there were giggles, there was moaning, there were bed springs creaking. And then the noises stopped for a little while, and then started up again.

It was about an hour later when she saw the boy get up and begin looking for his clothes. It was unlikely Esther was asleep, but she said nothing to the boy. Then the boy opened the door, walked out, and closed the door behind him.

* * *

After that, the only sounds Barbie could hear were the intermittent sounds of Esther snoring.

Barbie wished she could sleep as well, but that was impossible. She decided to try reciting some of the old prayers, *"Barukh atah Adonai Eloheinu melekh ha-olam shehakol..."* The words trailed off in her mind. What was the rest of it? She couldn't remember. Had it been that long? It couldn't be.

* * *

It was nearly 11 AM when Esther began to wake up. The sun was shining in through the window, but Esther was feeling too hung over to appreciate it.

After a while, Esther sat up, and then got up out of bed. She found a T-shirt and pulled it on to cover herself. Then she glanced over at where she had left Sheila Barbie on the chest of drawers.

There was nothing there. Esther went over to look. Sheila Barbie was not on the chest of drawers. She was not on the desk either.

Esther began to worry. She looked around every-where, until finally she saw... There was something there on the floor.

Esther kneeled down. There was Sheila Barbie. She had somehow fallen from the chest of drawers. And in the fall, Sheila Barbie's head had been snapped off from her body, and was lying there with her blonde hair splayed out and her blue eyes looking vacantly upwards.

Sheila Barbie's body was lying there too, with her legs askew, and with her Victoria's Secret white pant-ies peeking out silently from under her pink miniskirt.

TELLING STORIES,
OR HOW I STARTED WRITING PORN AND FOUND TRUE HAPPINESS

I SHOWED UP FOR CREATIVE WRITING CLASS at 7:00 p.m. on a Thursday evening. I still wasn't quite sure why I had gotten myself into this, and coming back into the building where I had gone to high school almost ten years earlier made the whole thing feel kind of depressing. It wasn't like I had been a great student. I graduated okay, and went on to community college, but then I flunked out, first semester.

I guess that's why, at age 27, I was working as a stock boy at Target. And no, calling it Tar-jay doesn't help. The job was boring, and I was going nowhere. And it wasn't like I was some hot-looking guy with loads of dates. Basically, my life was Target, pizza, and TV.

The write-up for the course told me that I *could* write, that I *had talent*, and this class would *change my life*. I wasn't sure I believed any of it, but on the plus side I had nothing to lose.

I was the first one there; I had had English class in this same room so I didn't have to wander around trying to find it. Pretty soon some other people began to arrive, including the teacher, Glynda.

Glynda's appearance made me think about pretending I had just noticed I was in the wrong class and heading for the door. She was plump, middle-aged, had her hair back in a ponytail, and was carrying a large plastic shopping bag—one of those recycled jobs they sell at supermarkets—stuffed with random folders and papers. With her gray sweater and brown skirt, she did not look remotely "creative."

There were only about a dozen of us in all, so Glynda suggested we pull our seats into a circle. "I'm Glynda," she began once we were all settled in. "I want you to understand this isn't like the usual kind of class where the teacher tells you stuff and you just listen. I'd like to think of this more like a little workshop where we are all sharing our ideas and learning from each other.

"I know some of you are nervous about being here and the whole idea of writing and having other people see what you have written. That's why it's so important for us to always look for the positive elements in what other class members write."

Some of the people had showed up with stuff they had already written, but for today, Glynda explained, she wanted to work on trust-building exercises to help the newcomers get started. You know, like the kind of thing where you fall backward in some room and "trust" a bunch of strangers to catch you.

The first exercise was for each person to take a piece of paper and write down three random objects.

"Don't try to be logical," Glynda emphasized, "just three random things." So I wrote down, "cat," "spaghetti," and "desert island." I saw some members of the class sitting there, staring blankly at their sheet of paper.

After a minute or so, Glynda said, "Now take these three objects and put them into a sentence." Oh shit. Why did I choose those? "The cat ate my spaghetti while I was on the desert island." I wanted a do-over, but Glynda was having none of it. "Okay class, just pass your papers around to me. Don't put your names on them—this is anonymous." I could see the looks of dismay on several faces, but Glynda seemed chipper as ever.

Wouldn't you know it? Mine was the first paper Glynda picked to read out to the class. "Okay class. Dwayne, let's see what you wrote: cat, spaghetti, desert island. And the sentence is, 'The cat ate my spaghetti while I was on the desert island.' So, any thoughts? Any comments? Remember, we're here to share positive suggestions."

No one said anything. But Glynda seemed delighted. "What an interesting choice of objects. And doesn't this sentence just paint a picture in your mind? Can't you see the cat eating the spaghetti, and all the sand and the ocean, and maybe a palm tree? I think there's all sorts of terrific stuff here. This is a *great* start."

I admit that when she read some of the other peoples' stuff, no one else's seemed quite as unusual and imaginative. But I still didn't see this as the beginning of a story.

* * *

For our next class, Glynda asked that we each write at least one page of something—anything we wanted—and email it to her before the next class.

It was nice she only wanted a page from us, but it wasn't helping. I couldn't come up with even one sentence. I was hopeless at this.

That weekend, however, I happened to pass by a garage sale and stopped to look. It was a pretty big sale with lots of old junk, as if someone had died and they were trying to get rid of their stuff. Anyway, I was looking around and spotted a box with some old copies of *The Saturday Evening Post*. You probably remember it as the magazine that had those covers by Norman Rockwell. I really liked them. And they had short stories in every issue. I didn't use to read them, but right now they might be helpful in giving me some ideas.

I bought about a dozen issues from the 50s and early 60s for 10¢ apiece and brought them back to my place.

The first story I spotted was pretty good. It was called, "Hey Fellah." It was written by somebody named Brian Wood. Anyway, it was about this guy who was an insurance agent and had a pretty boring job. So, one morning his wife cooked him his usual eggs over hard and bacon and toast and coffee. Only she didn't get the eggs quite hard enough so they were kind of gooey and runny. That really bugged him, but he didn't say anything, he just finished breakfast and went to his office.

This guy was usually pretty outgoing at work, like he would call out "Hey fellah" to everyone in the office, even the women, but today was not going well. One of his big-policy clients died in a car crash, so he would be losing a pretty sizable premium, and when his secretary handed him the latest sales figures from the past month, they looked alarmingly bad. And then, of course, the eggs. The more he thought about it, the more it bugged him. By the time lunch hour arrives, he's looking through the phone book, searching for ads for divorce lawyers. And of course, thinking about divorce only stresses him out even more. But then he looks over at the picture he keeps on his desk of him and his wife when they got married. And he realizes he loves her and he doesn't want to get divorced at all. And so, on the way home at the end of the day he stops off and buys her a surprise box of chocolates. And when he gets home and his wife opens the door for him, he hands her the box of chocolates and says, "Hey fellah!"

Now my idea had been to just look for ideas for stories I could write myself, but I knew I couldn't come up with anything this good, especially not in time for the next class. Instead, what I did was to type the whole story into my computer. But to make it more authentic, I just sent in the first part, up to where he's looking around in the phone book, so it would look like I was still working on it. Besides, that way I would get two weeks of material out of this one story.

I sent it in to Glynda without my name so she could share it with the class.

That following Wednesday, I got an email from Glynda with my story and seven others, all equally anonymous.

* * *

When class met again, we were down to six people, including Glynda. Apparently even a couple of the people who had written something and sent it in chickened out.

Glynda didn't seem surprised or upset. "A class like this gets smaller," she told us. "People get nervous, they get scared. But remember, I'm happy to have you show up even if you haven't written anything. If you keep coming, over time you'll start coming up with your own neat stuff."

I was a little nervous when she said that. I was worried that maybe she saw that what I had sent her was not "my own" neat stuff.

I needn't have worried. Class went swimmingly, so to speak. For one thing, with so many pieces to look at, we couldn't spend that much time on anyone's individual story. And in addition, a couple of the other pieces were so bad they would have made *me* look good—if I had actually written anything of my own.

Even though our names weren't on our stories, Glynda ended up having each of us read our own piece, so I got to see who was writing what. Some of them I don't remember at all, and some I'm still trying to forget.

There was one girl, Linda, who wrote this really boring story about breaking up with her boyfriend. I totally didn't care. For one thing I had never even had a girlfriend to break up with. So I couldn't come up with anything "positive" to say at all.

Another student was this smoking hot blonde girl from some Eastern European country. Her name was Natalya. The problem was she could barely speak English, and when it came to writing, I had no idea what her story was about. But damn she was hot. I was hoping she would keep coming to class.

And then there was this guy, Archie. He was kind of short and skinny with black hair that was thinning on top. It was hard to tell how old he was—he could have been a very old 20-something year old, or 40 or 50. He looked like someone who worked in a cubicle somewhere and didn't have a life. But I liked his story. I liked it a lot.

It was called "Tattoo." It was about this kind of wimpy guy who finally meets this really beautiful girl and somehow they end up falling in love and he marries her. Only it turns out she has a twin sister who looks just like her. And on his wedding night, when his bride undresses, he sees she has a tattoo of a butterfly on her left butt cheek. He's never seen her naked before, but now he sees this tattoo and he suddenly realizes he doesn't really know anything about her. And then he starts wondering if she is the twin he fell in love with, or if the sisters switched for the wedding and he's married to the wrong twin.

Anyway, this may not sound like much, but the way Archie wrote it, it was amazing. It just sang. You felt how the guy felt. You saw how the girl looked. And you couldn't stop thinking about that tattoo. Did the other sister have one too? Were they the same design? Were they on the same cheek?

I loved that story. But nobody else did. Linda, the girl with the sob story didn't think it was "sensitive" enough. (I could see she wanted to say it was stupid, but Glynda was looking at her with a warning look.) Natalya ended up talking about her tattoo on *her* butt, which was also pretty fascinating to me. I couldn't think of anything in particular to say about Archie's story except I liked it and that it was "cool." Glynda didn't seem to know what to say about it, except that it had "some interesting language" and she was looking forward to seeing his next story.

When it came to my story, Glynda was very impressed. "Wow, Dwayne, I really love how you use a detail like the runny eggs to start everything going in his head," she said. "And then things really do start spinning out of control, don't they? But I also like the idea of his saying 'Hey fellah' to everyone. You get a real picture of the kind of guy he is."

After class, I began thinking. I still had the ending of "Hey Fellah" to go, so I was covered for next week, but after reading Archie's story I wanted to do better. I needed to step it up. And I wasn't going to find what

I wanted in any of the issues of *The Saturday Evening Post* I had bought.

I wanted something newer, edgier, not from the 50s. I wanted to *grow* as a writer.

* * *

That Sunday, I took a bus into the city. I went down to an area where there were a couple of universities close to each other, with coffee shops and lots of students. It didn't take too long to find a run-down second-hand bookstore, called The Raven's Paradox, and I went in.

I asked the guy behind the counter if he had any old magazines with short stories. "What kind of stories?" he demanded. "Ya want porno, it's down in the basement, over in the back."

"No," I said. "Not porno. Just stories. Like in magazines that just print stories for people to read."

"Oh, right," he said. "Sure. I got a section of them downstairs, over on the left side. Literary journals, all that kind of stuff. I get people comin' in here for those. Not very often, though. Not like the porn."

I went downstairs. There were a couple of guys looking at the magazines in the back, as well as one female couple. I had the literary journal section to myself.

There were a lot of different magazine names, but usually only one or two issues of each. Most of them didn't stay in business long, I figured. I found a chair to settle down in and began thumbing through them pretty randomly. I found a couple of issues with potential—I was looking for issues with more than one story that might work. I ended up with four magazines—one *Kansas Prairie Literary Review*, one *Bayou Dustbin*, one *Elegies from the Swamp*, and one *Oestrus Rising*.

I took them upstairs to the man behind the counter. He looked at them. "Forty bucks," he said.

"What?" I said. "Forty bucks? For these old magazines no one will ever read?"

"What're you gonna do with them, kid? Read them? For the poetry? Bullshit. You want poems and shit you can copy and hand in in some writing class you're taking. Maybe impress some chick. Think you're the first one who ever thought of this? And you need these old magazines so no one can look them up online. Tell ya what. Thirty-five bucks for the four of them."

"Twenty," I said. "Or I walk."

"Listen kid, I know you wouldn't walk. But it's not worth hassling with you. Twenty it is."

I did walk. Back to the bus station. Too broke to stop off for a meal, or even a cup of coffee. But I had a stash a dealer would envy.

* * *

So here's the story I picked out to start with. It was from *Oestrus Rising*, but I'll leave out the author's name for reasons you can understand.

The name of the story was "Butterflies."

It's about this guy named Icarus. He has this idea about wanting to fly. And so, one day, he goes out to this big park overlooking the ocean and he sees all these butterflies. And he starts running after the butterflies and when he catches them, he pops them in his mouth and eats them. His thing is he figures if he eats a bunch of butterflies, he'll end up having dreams about flying.

That night, however, he doesn't dream about flying. He dreams about the butterflies being inside him, still alive. But since their wings have been dissolved in his stomach, they turn back into caterpillars and they start eating through his stomach and wandering around in his body. And he has this same dream every night, only it keeps getting worse. And finally, he has this dream where the caterpillars have reached his brain and are eating into it. And when he wakes up, he gets in his car and drives back out to the park. And he goes looking around and sees this cliff overlooking the ocean. And he runs over to the cliff and jumps off. And as he is heading over the cliff, he realizes...he is flying.

It was a really good story. I changed the name of the main character to Bob since I couldn't even figure out how to pronounce his original name. Besides, Bob began with "B" and so did butterflies, so I figured it would be kind of a link. And I had him bringing along a can of energy drink so when he catches the butterflies he would have something to wash them down with. I mean it seems like butterflies would be pretty hard to swallow. And there were a couple of words I didn't understand so I changed them or just left them out. After all, I wanted it to be *my* story as much as possible.

It was definitely a big step up from "Hey Fellah."

* * *

I sent in the second part of "Hey Fellah" as my piece for the second class, but mentally I was already way past that moment in my career.

The class seemed to like it, however. Glynda loved it, loved how the ending wrapped it all up. She also began talking about how it illustrated the classical unities of time and action.

The girl who had written about her breakup thought I should at least say what kinds of chocolates he was buying for her—like were they cream filled or solid or what? The Eastern European woman seemed to like that he loved his wife and went home with a present for her. But she too wanted to know more details about the chocolate. What brand? Were they expensive? Were they a "worthy" gift?

Archie liked it too. Said he liked how I could write that way about ordinary people in an ordinary setting and make us care about them.

"Actually," I told them, "this class has been encouraging me to try taking on new kinds of challenges, so the story I'm working on for next week is pretty different."

Glynda beamed like a proud mother hen.

* * *

On the way out of class I managed to time it so that Archie and I walked out together.

"I really liked your story, Dwayne," Archie said. "I never know if my characters feel real or not. But your guy was totally real." Then he added, "How long did it take you to write it?

I was taken by surprise by his question. I wasn't sure what the best thing was to tell him. "Well," I said, "I guess I had been working on it for a while. I mean I think the idea started for me when I was having breakfast at Denny's a month or two ago and I ordered eggs over hard and they came out runny. I don't like to send things back or complain so I just ate them. But it made me mad. As for the rest, I've never been married or anything, so I had to make that part up. When I was a kid my dad sold insurance—although he sold policies to companies that owned hotels and big office buildings. I had been thinking about it and I guess I started writing the story when I signed up for the course. I couldn't figure out the ending for a while. That's why I had to do it in two parts. How about you? How long did it take for you to write 'Tattoo'?"

I could see how shy Archie was. It was like he would have loved to be a turtle and just pull his head back into his shell rather than talk about himself. But I guess what I said had reassured him somewhat.

"Gosh," he started, "I don't know how long it took. It seems like forever. I mean I couldn't tell the twins apart, so it was very confusing. And I still don't know if the other twin also had a tattoo or even whether he married the twin he thought he was marrying. I don't really feel like I finished it right. I don't even like to talk about writing. That's why I'm taking this class. I just don't feel like I know what I'm doing."

"Well," I told him. "*I* liked it. Even if it *was* kind of rough around the edges. I'll bet if you keep working at it, you'll get better."

"That's really nice of you to say," Archie told me. "I appreciate it. And I'm looking forward to seeing your new story next week."

"Will *you* have another story ready for next week?" I asked him. He hadn't brought in anything this week.

"I hope so," Archie said. "I've been writing stories for years. It's just that I never think they're any good."

"Well, be sure and show us another one this next time," I said. "Do it for me."

* * *

Well, what with the positive feedback about my first story and my own excitement about the literary magazines and this whole new world I was discovering, I decided it was time for me to take the next step. I wanted to publish something. After all, wasn't that what this was all about? Creating a new me?

And besides, Archie's story had inspired me.

I wasn't sure where to start. I didn't want to go to the literary magazines. If I sent in something they recognized... I figured it was probably a small world. And besides, they didn't pay anything. And while it wasn't *all* about the money, I did want to be treated like a professional.

Eventually I found myself looking at lists of "adult" magazines that used fiction. I figured no one from class would see anything there, and I was sure the people at those magazines never read any of the literary journals.

I really wanted to send in something original. But it was still too early for that. "Hey Fellah" wasn't quite right. But "Tattoo"... I figured I would change some things around, make it a little different, add some stuff.

But the thing was, the more I read it, the more I realized I couldn't change anything. Every time I tried, it seemed like it just clunked.

So finally, having spent many hours on this problem I made my own editorial decision. I would send it in as it was. But since it was an adult magazine, I had a feeling I shouldn't use my own name either. So I came up with a fake name, created a new email account to go with it, and sent in the story.

When I was done, I felt good. I was taking charge of my life for a change.

* * *

I thought my new story for the class was a big step up. And I figured everyone else would be impressed with how my style was evolving.

But that wasn't how it went. Linda thought the idea of eating butterflies was just gross. "Ewww. I don't even want to think about it." Natalya, the hot one, felt it didn't make any sense. "People in my country don't do that kind of thing. Not any of it."

I could see Glynda was trying to find something encouraging and positive to say. But all she could come up with was that it was "certainly more complex" than "Hey Fellah," but she wasn't sure how she was supposed to relate to the character. But it was important for all of us to try new things, even if not everything worked the first time.

* * *

After class Archie caught up with me.

"Your new story was pretty interesting," he said. "It *was* really different... But I don't know... I guess I kind of liked your first story better. I still find myself thinking about it."

I could see Archie had something on his mind, so I waited for him to come out with it.

"Dwayne... have you ever..." He hesitated. "Have you ever sent anything out to a magazine or anything for publication? I've been wondering about it, but I'm really scared about getting rejected."

"Well," I told him. "I did try sending some stuff out a few years ago. I mean back then I wasn't nearly as good as I am now. And I got rejected every time. But the worst one was when some editor wrote me a letter telling me I was an awful writer and I should do everyone a favor and never write another word again."

"It was pretty brutal," I continued. "I think I would have rather had someone beat me up physically. I mean some of these editors really aren't nice at all. And you never know what they're going to do. It was so bad I haven't tried sending in anything since then."

Archie looked shaken. "Oh my," he said. "I don't think I could handle that at all."

"I don't want to discourage you," I said. "I'm pretty sure with a few more years of writing classes you'll have something ready to send out."

"Well, thanks," Archie said, "for telling me about your experience. And I'm glad you liked my first story. I just can't seem to come up with another one yet. But I'm going to keep trying."

* * *

I figured I had the Archie situation under control. I was pretty pleased with myself for my quick thinking. He wasn't going to even think about sending in any of his work for a long time—maybe ever.

It was only a day or two later I got an email in response to my own submission.

Dear Dumbass,

I shouldn't even be talking to you seeing as how dumb you are, but I'm gonna tell you, JUST ONCE, what you need to do for next time.

We don't pay extra for style, but your story caught my attention because most of the people who send us stuff can barely write whole sentences. And you have a storyline here with some real potential for us. One guy, two girls. And they're twins. And one has a tattoo. You got plenty of room to work with here.

So, here's the deal. GIRLZ is a PUSSY maga-
zine. We sell pussy. By the boatload. The girls
in the centerfold have their legs wide open and
are pulling their pussies open. Every photo-
graph we print has pussy in it. And so—be sure
you're following me here—so do all the stories
in our magazine.

I'm giving you one more chance. You rewrite
this story with pussy in it. Sex, sex and more
sex. Got it? Jerking off, blow jobs, sex on top,
sex on the bottom, doggy style, three-ways,
everything you got. Everything you've always
wanted to do but never got the chance. Like all
those poor assholes who buy our magazine.

If you can do this, we got a deal. If not, I
block your email and you're out for good.
Bernie
Sr. Fiction Editor

* * *

I wasn't sure what to think. Was it sort of a non-
rejection rejection? But he was offering me a chance.
To do some more writing—and get paid for it! All I
had to do was stick in a bunch of sex scenes. Like
those ads on TV used to say, "Even a caveman could
do it!"

That night I got to work. I decided to set myself a
goal. A minimum of five sex scenes, but try for ten.
Bernie had even given me a list. And I was sure I could
add to it with my own vivid imagination and writerly
flair.

On a practical level, I ended up writing only one scene each night. For technical reasons. I don't want to talk about that part of the writing process. Let's just call it a professional secret.

* * *

This was great. I was a real for sure writer. A real magazine editor had asked me to write for them.

I couldn't tell the class about this, of course. So I just talked vaguely about how some of my friends liked my stories. But inside I was beginning to feel just a bit superior.

* * *

After the way the class had reacted to my story about the guy and the butterflies, I decided to go back to *The Saturday Evening Post* for my next story. I found a story about some guy who went around doing secret good deeds for people. It was called, "Have a Nice Day." It was set in a small town and so when he started doing these good deeds it had like a ripple effect—the people he did secret good deeds for decided to do secret good deeds for other people and pretty soon the whole town had become this really happy place.

I mean it was a good enough story on its own, but I had something I wanted to add to it. So I put in a bit where this guy found a story someone else had written and he sent it into a magazine and they accepted it and the guy who had written the story had been afraid to send it in and now it was published and everything so he was really happy.

Well, you know the class loved the story. And everyone loved my bit about the guy sending in the story.

And I felt extra good because that was the part I had written myself.

* * *

I had to wait two weeks before I heard back from Bernie. Another email.

> *Hey Dumbass,*
>
> *What the fuck is wrong with you? Have you ever gotten laid in your entire worthless life? These sex scenes are the lamest shit I've ever seen.*
>
> *If I didn't have someone here to rewrite the sex scenes, I wouldn't be writing to you at all. But I have a guy who can bang out some new stuff in a day. It ain't fucking rocket science. It's just sex.*
>
> *Against my better judgment we're going to print your story in the next issue—with our guy's sex scenes. I wouldn't bother with you at all, but like I said, you got a good story here.*
>
> *I'll be mailing you our payment of $100, in cash, to the address you gave me. I'll address it to "Occupant" since I'm sure the mailman won't know who the hell Harry Hardcox is.*

My suggestion to you is, go out and spend it
on porno mags and learn how to write sex
scenes. You do that, and send us good stories,
and we got a deal going.
　I still don't get how you can write such a
good story and such lousy sex scenes. Remem-
ber—this is your last chance.
Bernie
Sr. Fiction Editor

Wow. This was great. I was actually going to get paid. Real money. And he wanted me to send him more.

I liked Bernie. Very down to earth. And he always had practical suggestions for me to follow.

The plain brown envelope arrived a week later. Two fifties enclosed.

Now I know $100 isn't like winning the lottery or anything. But when you're working in a minimum wage, dead-end job, it feels like a million bucks. It feels great. Pure green self-esteem.

* * *

I know what you're thinking. About the sex scenes I had written. And the worst part is it's true. I mean I'm not exactly ugly or anything, but I guess you would describe me as kind of a nerd. You know, like being a nerd is kind of like being a geek but without being smart.

And the fact is I liked girls, and I had kissed a few girls in my time, but none had ever wanted to come back for more.

I guess I was what some of those marketing guys would call an aspirational heterosexual. "Aspirational" is a term they use for some of the clothing lines in the store. I like to add to my vocabulary whenever I can.

But I knew Bernie was expecting more from me. So on Saturday I took a bus back into the city and went back to The Raven's Paradox. I headed downstairs and went to the rear section. There were a couple of other guys looking around, but none of us made eye contact. In any case, I wasn't like them. I was here on business.

I had to look pretty hard to find magazines with actual stories in them, but I came up with five of them that had the kinds of stories I needed to get me started.

The guy behind the counter recognized me from before. He looked at my magazines and said, "So, you finally decided to go for the real thing, eh?

"This is for research," I told him.

I don't know if he believed me. He wanted twenty-five bucks for the magazines, but settled for fifteen.

* * *

When I got home, I read through all of them.

They weren't good stories at all. But I had to admit the sex scenes were better than mine. I wasn't sure I was ready to write new sex scenes on my own, so I decided to just type out the hottest sex scenes into my computer, along with a title word for what kind of scene it was—jerking off, fucking, anal, threesomes, etc.

I was being really methodical and professional. I now had a ready to go reference file of sex action scenes I could plug into the right moments in any story. I mean the truth is the sex stuff was mostly pretty generic. What made my work special was the story itself.

* * *

After that, life kind of settled into a routine. I kept on coming up with new stories for class each week. I wanted to do more with the literary stuff, but every time I used one of those stories the other members of the class didn't like it. So I ended up pretty much sticking with *The Saturday Evening Post* stuff. But it bothered me. I felt like the class was keeping me from reaching my full potential.

I kept waiting for Archie to come in with a new story, but he didn't. Week after week he just came in and sat there, hardly saying anything at all.

Fortunately, I had found a few literary stories I felt would work for GIRLZ. With my bank of sex scenes, I filled them full of scenes that left nothing to anyone's imagination.

It also helped that on my next trip to The Raven's Paradox, the guy behind the counter saw me and called me over. "Hey," he said, "I got something here you might like." From beneath the counter, he pulled out a copy of GIRLZ. "They got a story in here that sounds like it's right up your alley—kind of like that literary stuff only full of sex scenes."

I looked inside. Sure enough, there was my story. They had renamed it "Tattoo on My Wife's Ass" but it was my story. And I had to admit the sex scenes were pretty good, and I know I wouldn't have thought of some of them.

The guy charged me ten bucks for GIRLZ, but he let me pick out two more porno magazines for free. I also sprang for a couple more literary magazines. My stock of stories was running low.

What a day. Seeing my own story in print. I wanted to read it on the bus ride home, but I settled for the literary magazines so as not to look like a pervert.

* * *

I was on a real high. I was a published writer, making real money. And I was coming up with a constant flow of stories.

When I went to class, however, Archie was waiting for me in the hall. He looked pretty upset.

"Dwayne, can I talk to you for a moment?" he asked. "I don't know what to do, and you're the only one I can talk to."

"Sure," I said. There was plenty of time before class, and Archie motioned me around the corner so no one else would see us.

"Well, you remember when I was asking you about submitting stories that night?" he said. "And you told me about what had happened to you?"

I nodded.

"Well, after that I wasn't going to try to send in anything at all. But then that next week when you had the story with the guy doing the secret good deed about sending in someone else's story and how happy the guy was when it was published? Anyway, that story you wrote kind of changed my mind and I decided to go ahead and give it a try after all."

"And?" I said, a bit warily. "What happened?"

"Well," Archie continued, "I looked around for some little magazines that printed stories. These days that pretty much means the literary journals. They don't pay, but I thought maybe they would print my story. So I found one called *Arkanumdrum* and sent 'Tattoo' in to them. I figured it would take them a long time to get back to me."

I waited for him to get to the point.

"Well, it didn't take long. It was like two days later and I get a very angry email from this guy Bernard who is the editor. And he's asking me what I'm trying to pull off here. He says he talked to another guy he knows who is the editor of another magazine and this story is a rip-off of something they published last month. And he tells me if I ever try sending them anything again, he'll sue me for fraud and plagiarism."

Holy shit.

Archie paused for a moment, then went on. "I didn't believe it, but he mentioned it was in some magazine called GIRLZ—that's like 'girls' only with a 'z' on the end—and it had been out on the stands for a month. I didn't know anything about GIRLZ, but there was this one guy in my office who is kind of into, you know, 'adult' stuff, and I asked him about it. And anyway, it turns out he has that very issue in his desk drawer in his cubicle."

I could almost feel Archie shudder as he told me about all this. But he went on. "Now I don't know if you've ever heard of GIRLZ magazine. All I can say is it's pretty...*unsavory*. But there was this story—the title was a little different and it was a different author's name, and there were all sorts of sex scenes in it I sure didn't write, and *couldn't* have written—but it was *my* story."

He looked drained. "What do you think I should do?" he asked me. "Do you think I should hire a detective? Do you think I need to hire a lawyer in case they try to sue me?"

"Wow," I said. "That's one weird story. If it were me, I think I'd just forget about it. Like I did when that editor told me to not write anything ever again. I mean, it's not any fun, but what can you do?"

Archie's shoulders slumped. He looked at me again and said, "Thanks. Thanks for listening to me. This has all just been really upsetting to me."

"But," he added, "at least I did bring in a new story for this class."

* * *

Archie's new story was a doozy. Kind of, at least.

It had to do with this guy named Herb. And it turns out he sells insurance. Only instead of sitting around in an office, Herb goes knocking on people's doors to find customers. So like he comes to this one house—it's a real big fancy house—and he knocks on the door. And this woman opens the door, only she's wearing this short pink robe. And she is an absolute knockout—a California blue-eyed blonde type with an amazing smile and this great body. And Herb tells her he's going around the neighborhood to see if anyone needs any insurance. She tells him she doesn't really know, why doesn't he come out to the pool and talk to her sisters with her? So they go through the living room and out some French doors to the backyard pool. And there are her two sisters. And no, they're not twins. Or triplets. Or anything. They're just sisters. Sister number two has long dark hair and dark eyes and looks sophisticated as all hell, even though she is in this tiny little bikini. And the third sister is this redhead. I won't even bother. You already know she's hot.

Anyhow, even though Herb is wearing this crumpled suit and isn't any kind of a knockout in any case, they invite him to grab a chair and tell them about insurance while they splash around.

Oh man, this is writing itself. I'm plugging in the sex scenes as I go. Three-way, four-way, girl on girl, girl on girls...

And they're all making eyes at him and flirting with him. Like it's some kind of contest. I keep thinking of Goldilocks and the 3 Bears, only it's Herb and the 3 Babes.

And they're all rubbing suntan lotion over each other and untying their tops to get a better tan. And you're wondering what Herb is going to do. I mean this could drive a guy totally nuts. So he's pulling policies out of his briefcase and reading from them. And one of the sisters asks does he have a card?

Of course he does. So Herb stands up to get out his wallet. And then, when he opens his wallet to get out a card, he sees this picture of his wife that he has in there. And he realizes it's nearly dinner-time and he's going to be late and he shouldn't really be here anyway.

What? Where did this come from? Archie, what the fuck just happened? This is *not* an Archie story.

And yeah, Herb grabs his stuff and runs for the door and gets in his car and drives off. And the three sisters are just laughing like hell.

Archie, I can't use this. C'mon, give me something cool, something weird. Not this shit.

I had left my coat on a desk at the back of the room, and had to go back to get it when class ended. When I looked around again, Archie was gone.

* * *

I never did know anything about what Archie did, or where he worked, or where he lived. He never came to class again. I never saw him again.

Actually, there were only two more weeks of class and after that I never felt like signing up for another writing class. I had graduated. I was ready to be a grown-up.

It turns out I've developed a kind of relationship with Bernie. He still calls me "Dumbass," but he's nicer about it. He knows he needs me, and I know it too.

He's watched me grow artistically. He doesn't have to have someone else rewrite the sex scenes. In fact, he hardly rewrites anything at all.

He's upped my pay to $250 a story. It's still not much, but I have my day job, and my writing income is all in cash and tax-free. And now that I have my system in place, I'm turning them out faster—usually one a month, sometimes more, although then he has to farm it out to one of his other publications.

And with the extra money and with my Target employee discount, I went to the clothing department and bought some new duds. Nothing real fancy, just stuff that would make me look a little more hip and a little cooler. I mean with the new way my life was going, I needed to start dressing the part.

* * *

The other day this girl named Loretta, she's a cashier here at Target, came by while I was stocking shelves in the electronics department. She's kind of cute—not like super-hot or anything, but really nice. Anyway, she started talking to me and was saying how I seemed different lately, more confident or something. And she liked the new clothes. She said maybe I'd end up being a manager someday.

She also told me she had broken up with her boyfriend a while back and asked if I'd like to maybe get together and hang out sometime.

I'd like that a lot. Hell, maybe I could even write some new sex scenes based on real experience sometime. Or maybe not. I kind of think I'd want to keep that private. Just the two of us.

WOULD YOU DIE FOR ME?

"WOULD YOU DIE FOR ME?" she asked him one afternoon.

Abe was sitting on the sofa grading some student papers. She was cleaning up, putting stray books back on the bookshelves and making the motions of dusting here and there. She was wearing an ordinary dress of hers, nothing special or seductive.

At first the question flew by him as he continued marking up the essay he was working on.

"Would you die for me?" she asked him again, not letting it go.

He stopped for a moment and looked at her.

"What on earth are you talking about?" he asked. "Die for you? What does that even mean?"

"Just what I said, 'Would you die for me?' It's a simple question."

"No, it's not simple. It doesn't even make sense."

"Of course it does. Let's say you were sitting here in the living room and there was a knock at the door and you answered it and this strange skeleton-man in a black robe with a black hood was there and said to you, 'I am Death, and I am here to see Kaley.' Would you say, 'Oh, she's in the kitchen,' or would you say, 'She's not here, won't you take me instead?'

"Which would you do?"

Kaley had been a student in one of his classes the previous semester. She had run into him on campus about a month ago. They had been dating for three weeks, and for the past week she had essentially moved in, spending all her time at his place.

"I'm asking because I am on a quest to find a true love. And that means someone who would die for me, no?

"If you would not want to die for me, then what am I to you? You say you love me, but I believe I am no more than, what would you say, a 'divertissement'?"

Had he told her he loved her? He couldn't remember. Maybe in bed one night. But that sort of thing is different. Heat of the moment and all that.

Now she wanted him to *die* for her? What the fuck?

He knew in any advice column anywhere he would be told in no uncertain terms that this was a Red Flag moment. A sign this relationship, whatever it was, made no sense and it was time for him—them?—to call it quits. Actually, for him to run like hell and not look back. He knew that, but at the same time, that thought made him anxious.

Was she spectacular in bed? That wasn't really what he would say about it. It wasn't about acrobatics, or the latest sex tips from *Cosmo*. But she was, when the moment was right, seductive, and addictive.

In a different relationship this whole thing might have been an excuse for him to put down his grading and lead her into the bedroom.

But that wasn't it. There was no hint of sex about this moment. In some way she always seemed to ration sex with him. He wanted her, but he could only have her on her terms. When she wanted, and not before, and not after.

While some of his previous girlfriends had been fun but casual, with Kaley, he always had this feeling he hadn't made love to her enough yet. He wasn't finished. He needed more.

He had no idea whether she needed him at all. What the hell did dying for her have to do with it? Would that change things? Would it make her insatiable with lust for him, or would she stay exactly the same even as he had promised to die for her?

Did she have a pack of previous lovers, all of whom had been ready to die for her? Would they march in lockstep like lemmings and leap into the sea?

"Look, this just isn't making any sense to me right now. No, you are not a 'diversion,' but I have to grade these papers. We can talk some more later on."

He picked up the stack of papers again and went back to the one he had left off reading. He was trying to concentrate, but these were freshman essays and dull to begin with. He found himself wondering, suppose she needed a kidney, would he give her one? Even something as simple as that didn't make any real sense at this stage of their relationship. Why was he thinking of kidneys? Then again, he did have two of them, and so maybe he would give her a kidney. How about an eye, or retina or cornea or whatever it is that people donate? That could really get in his way. He knew he couldn't give her a hand or a foot or anything like that, which made it a little easier to sidestep the issue.

But he knew that wasn't what she was asking. It wasn't medical. She wanted him to *die* for her. You know, the big one. Death. Six-feet-under Death. Or at least be willing to die. What the fuck? Was she maybe part of some satanic cult that had human sacrifice as part of their rituals?

Abe doggedly returned his attention to the papers in his lap and finished grading the one he had been working on. Then he moved on to the next. As he sometimes did—actually as he often did—he looked through the pile of papers to see which would be quickest and easiest to grade and which would be the biggest pain, and he moved the easier ones to the top. That way there would be less time left to read the hard ones and he would just get through them without spending too much time deliberating and fine-tuning their grades.

Faced with the easier papers, he began to make progress and started to feel a little bit better. Maybe she would've forgotten this whole silly business by the time he finished with the stack. It was Friday afternoon, and once he finished, he would be looking at an open weekend to spend with Kaley doing...what? Why couldn't this whole thing just be simpler, more straightforward, more...convenient? He had enough drama dealing with students and their grades every week, couldn't he have a relationship that offered some time off from drama?

It didn't look that way.

Besides, Kaley was 14 years younger than him. That was fine for a night or two, or even a week or two, but it didn't look promising for a relationship. Shouldn't he be looking for something, or someone, more appropriate? He wasn't getting any younger, and his first book was with an academic publisher and was going through final edits, and his prospects for tenure were looking pretty decent. Wasn't it time to think about being a grown-up? Not that he was in any real rush on that score, but still...

And so, what the hell was he doing with Kaley?

Kaley had turned 20 a month ago, just before they started seeing each other. She was one of hundreds of coeds he had taught over the past five and a half years at the University. In terms of looks and general intelligence she was more or less interchangeable with dozens of them. There were always two or three or four who would catch his eye each semester, who he would think about and sometimes even fantasize about. He had ended up dating some of them, but it had never turned into anything like this.

Kaley was tall and thin, with long black hair and deep blue eyes made even bigger and more arresting by the dark eyeliner she always wore. In class, her choice of clothes was sort of quirky retro hipster, which helped make her at least appear to be intellectually-minded. She wasn't a flashy knockout, the kind guys would turn and follow with their eyes as she walked down the street, but in an academic setting, where the emphasis was more on the combination of looking intelligent as well as looking good, she was in her element.

When she had taken his survey course in British and American poetry, he had been sure she harbored some sort of natural affinity for poetry and understood it intuitively, even though the papers she had submitted never really lived up to that assessment. Maybe it wasn't that she had an affinity for poetry, but that she embodied his idea of poetry—something darkly attractive, sensual, and always with a depth that lay hidden from others. He was sure there was something about her that was important, and he found himself almost desperate to understand what it was.

So was all this that was happening this afternoon not the Red Flag it looked like, but rather some kind of proof there was a mystery here that he must pursue—even if, as he thought in the manner of his beloved romantic poets, he had to pursue it unto death?

This was not an entirely unhappy thought. It certainly felt more interesting than simply living out a career getting stale teaching the same courses, books, plays, and poems to an audience of students whose hairstyles and clothing fashions changed from year to year but whose minds didn't.

* * *

When Abe had returned to grading his papers, Kaley had gone to the kitchen to start making dinner. When she had time, he had learned, she was a very good cook, willing to put up with all the peeling and chopping and other labor that real cooking required.

By the time he had finished grading the last paper, he could smell dinner cooking and heard Kaley calling him into the kitchen. She had set their places at the table at one end of the kitchen, and had opened one of the bottles of wine to let it breathe. She had also changed her outfit and was now wearing a red wrap dress he had never seen before.

"Don't worry, I'm not going to ask you about dying for me over dinner," she told him. He poured the wine into their glasses while she served up salad for both of them. "Hold on," she said, "I just need to drain the pasta while it's still al dente."

The bottle of wine she had chosen from the half dozen or so he had on hand was, in fact, the very most expensive of all of them, one he had been planning to save for a special occasion. Well, he supposed, this was just going to be a special occasion.

The wine was good, almost worth what he had paid for it. The salad was simple but fresh, and when they had finished that first course, she got their main course for them. It was homemade spaghetti Bolognese, made from scratch.

The Bolognese was amazing, probably the best he could remember ever eating, even at an upscale Italian restaurant. He would've had seconds, but she had only made enough for one helping for each of them.

For dessert, she had bought a small box of Godiva chocolates. They had finished the bottle of wine by now, and so they decided to take the chocolates into the living room along with some not-so-small snifters of brandy.

Abe couldn't believe how good the meal had been and how relaxed he felt sitting here on the sofa with Kaley eating Godiva chocolate and sipping brandy. Was it the wine, or maybe the brandy, but something about the situation was going to his head.

That was when Kaley looked at him and said, "Oh, by the way, I added something to the spaghetti sauce. I had an extra cap of psilocybin at my place and I went ahead and added it to the sauce while I was cooking. It's not that much, I mean that was just one hit split between the two of us. Not really a trip, maybe more like just a little cruise. I thought it would make the evening more interesting."

What? What the hell? On the other hand, Abe had tripped before, so he wasn't totally freaked out by the idea, but it'd been a while. And was doing psilocybin with Kaley after all that talk this afternoon really something he needed to be doing right now?

He couldn't remember if there was anything people used to block a psilocybin high, so despite his misgivings, he figured he might as well go with it. Meanwhile, he could begin to feel the telltale twitches in his mind as the effects began to come on.

Well, here he was, sitting on the sofa with Kaley, and starting to trip. He looked at her, and began to see her hair shimmering and he felt himself just staring into the blue of her eyes as if they were some sort of a luminous portal into another universe.

Certainly different from spending the evening watching TV.

He heard Kaley saying something. She was asking about his book, the one the publisher was editing now.

His book... It had felt so important when he was writing it: *The Romantic Conundrum: Idealism, Confusion and Chaos in the Correspondence of the Romantic Poets.* It was his ticket to tenure, and maybe a chance to get recognized in his field. A bright young man on his way up. But at this moment even trying to remember what it was about was beyond him, and he was wondering why he had ever bothered with it in the first place. It all sounded like such boring and pretentious crap. And no, he couldn't tell her about it. He probably couldn't even put the title together for her.

He sat there, saying nothing, just staring at her.

* * *

Kaley sat there for a few moments letting him stare into her eyes. Then she took his hand in hers and began leading him out of the living room and down the hall to the bedroom.

As he followed her down the hallway, he saw the red dress slip from her shoulders and fall to the floor. She was not wearing anything underneath. He somehow managed to avoid stepping on the pool of red fabric as he followed her.

There were candles already lit as they entered the bedroom and she turned around to look at him. He had seen her naked before of course, but this was different. His musings about her? Her body, standing there before him, *was* poetry, in all its beauty and mysteriousness.

It was hard to remember how he got his own clothes off, but it didn't matter. Standing there before her, both of them naked, he felt the echoes of Adam and Eve, and the temptations of sin—*"Would you die for me?"*

Why *did* Adam eat the apple? For love? For sex? Was the apple simply the drug he took to have a good time, to hell with the consequences?

There he was, overthinking again, working too hard to figure out the naked mystery that stood there right in front of him, a mystery that for now demanded no thinking at all.

She stepped forward and kissed him, her naked body pressed tightly against his. She had never kissed him this way before; in the past, he was always aware that somehow she was holding something back, and that something was what he wanted most, why he could never get enough of her.

This time he felt the passion from her he had been longing for. As they fell onto the bed, he felt a new kind of sensuality that was all-embracing and locked the two of them together into a new kind of entity. There were, for the first time, no boundaries between them, there was no separation. It *was* like being launched into the Garden of Eden—a place of perfect innocence, a place where flowers grew where they lay and beauty was everywhere.

He had taught the poetry of the ages for all these years, but for the first time he was *living* it. He was embracing the universe, he was embracing the wondrous ways of God.

He had no way of telling how long they did all the things that they did. He seemed to recall her asking him several times, as if from afar, "Would you die for me?" But he couldn't tell if it was her or simply a voice in his head.

It still made no sense to him. And he had no time to think about it. This was a time for something else.

Finally, they fell back together, side-by-side, arms and hands holding each other. Neither said anything. They just looked at each other silently, and he felt as if they were welded together, in a way that could not come undone. He stared into her eyes as he had earlier on the sofa. There was still that sense of looking into the cosmos, but now there was something else as well. Was it some kind of sadness?

He was still wondering as he fell fast asleep.

* * *

When Abe woke up in the morning, the sun was beginning to shine through the blinds. He looked over at the space beside him in the bed. There was no one there.

He listened for sounds of Kaley in the kitchen, or taking a shower, or maybe in the living room puttering about. There was nothing.

What the hell?

Alarmed, he got out of bed to check on where she was. The bathroom was empty, the kitchen was empty, the living room was empty.

Her red dress was gone from the floor of the hallway, and as he began to look around, everything of hers—her toothbrush, the book she had been reading, even all the little tchotchkes she had been leaving around the apartment to mark her territory—everything was gone.

When he went into the kitchen again, he spotted a piece of paper on the dining table. It was a note in Kaley's handwriting:

> *Dear Abe,*
>   *Last night was beautiful, it was almost everything I could've hoped for. But you are not the true love I am looking for.*
>   *That makes me very sad. I truly did hope you were. But you will be fine. There'll be another, and then another, and then another. And perhaps one day you will understand, or perhaps not. I am not sure which is the better fate.*
>   *Kaley*

* * *

In late spring, the English department reviewed Abe's new book and the committee unanimously voted to award him tenure. Abe's future was safe and secure, and he intended to enjoy it.

He had always loved being the budding rock star professor on campus. In his classes, the young women would fix their gaze on him, and when they had a question, they would raise their hand and say, "Sir?" They looked up to him and admired him in a way that girls had never done when he was an undergraduate. Now, at a time when his bigshot peers in college had gone on to business school or law school and corporate or professional careers, he was still on campus, surrounded by beautiful and attentive young women. Yes, he was older now, but fortunately he still looked young and never imagined himself as being "too old" for them. He knew, he saw, other professors a decade or even two or three decades older than him still hanging out with coeds as if they had discovered the fountain of eternal youth for themselves.

Would I die for her? He had no time for that. Death was not welcome in his life. Death was the stuff of unpleasant diseases and silly accidents. There were too many other things on his mind.

Would I die for her—that was about *her*, about the fact that she was looking for someone who would do anything for her, give up anything for her. It was pure Romanticism. It wasn't about actual dying.

Sure, death was inevitable, it comes to all of us, but was the price of being with someone ultimately about being willing to face the inevitability of death while living an ordinary life? Did Adam understand the pact he was making when he took the apple from Eve? Was it love that drove him, or lust? If he had refused the apple, would God have gone ahead and given him a replacement Eve on the condition they have no sex ever?

If "growing up" included death as part of the package, he had no plans to grow up ever. And yet...

What Kaley had offered him was what Eve had offered Adam. Except instead of an apple, she had given him psilocybin and the poetry of life. And he *was* tempted. And then the temptation had disappeared, leaving him wondering about his decision or his lack of decision.

* * *

Abe found himself thinking of Kaley more and more often these days. He had married three months ago, a month before he was about to turn 48. She, his wife, was 26. She had been a grad student in one of his seminars and things had gone on from there. She was attractive and smart and ready to fit into her life as a professor's wife. She had once thought she might turn her dissertation into a book, but now she thought more about starting a family.

There was still some awkwardness at faculty parties; the male faculty mostly understood and some even envied him, the female faculty understood all too well and resented both of them.

Abe enjoyed the fact that his wife was still young and hot. At the same time, he had the nagging feeling he had settled, settled for someone good enough— even very good enough—while he still could. He was not *old* yet, he reminded himself, and he probably could've kept going another decade in the life he had been leading. But then what? The equation would've been different then. He would've been too old to do what he was doing now, even if what he was doing now marked his acceptance of his mortality and his entrance into the pedestrianism of life.

Even now, he could see the tiny cracks around the edges. If things felt awkward when he brought his wife to faculty gatherings, he found himself feeling just as awkward around his wife's young friends, and especially the bright, hip, and athletic young men who formed her real age cohort.

He found himself feeling out of place and time and confused about things he had taken for granted. And he found himself thinking again of Kaley. "Would I die for her?" he asked himself. "Yes...yes" he found himself repeating, almost like a mantra, "I would die for her...over and over and over..."

NIGHT OF THE CHIMPS

*"She was a world-famous scientist, but
here in the jungle, she was also...a woman..."*

IT WAS MIDMORNING when Rachel first saw the cloud of dust in the distance. In that direction, there was flat grassland with a wide, unobstructed view; on the other side of her was the edge of the forest where the chimps she was observing lived. The sun had already moved from warm to hot, and her chimps were busy with their usual daytime activities—looking for food, grooming each other, and generally hanging out. A few were keeping a wary eye out for predators, and they too took notice of the cloud of dust that indicated something coming their way.

It was nearly a half hour before the Jeep finally pulled up and parked near Rachel's tent. The driver was a man wearing the same kind of outfit as Rachel—a tan khaki short-sleeved shirt, khaki shorts, and a pair of leather hiking boots. He was wearing a brimmed hat to ward off the sun, but he was heavily tanned, the kind of deep tan that comes from a life spent living and working outdoors in the veldt.

Rachel had been working in Africa for 20 years, and had spent the past ten years studying the lives and habits of chimpanzees. She was used to spending months, even as much as a year, without seeing another white person, and in fact rarely saw any other people at all. She was hardly desperate for company, but she enjoyed the break in her routine that an occasional visitor offered.

"Jack. Jack Riley." The man offered his hand as he introduced himself. "I know who you are, Dr. Anderson. I'm a long-time admirer of your work."

"Call me Rachel, please," she said. She shook his hand and looked him over. He was 50-ish? 60-ish? Maybe, for that matter, in his mid-40s. Life out here had kept him in shape in a way that made him seem like part of the landscape.

"I'm heading out to do a U.N. wildlife survey," Jack said. "I heard you were out here, and I thought I'd take the opportunity to meet you and drop off some extra supplies."

Rachel had learned to be pretty self-sufficient, but some more rice and beans, and especially some cigarettes, would be nice to have.

Jack set up his own tent a little way from hers; it made sense to spend the night here before heading out again in the morning.

When he was done, Rachel began showing him the chimpanzee troop she was observing. Although she herself had long since become friendly with the chimps, and they didn't mind her walking around among them, Jack was new and an outsider, so the two of them stayed at a distance while she told him her names for the different members of the group and explained their hierarchy and pointed out the alpha males.

Jack was very interested in all of this, and asked lots of questions about social dynamics within the troop. Rachel gave him detailed descriptions of the individual personalities of the different chimps, male and female, and even the young chimps.

After a while, Rachel brought out two folding chairs so they could just sit and watch and talk.

It was good to talk. Rachel hadn't had any visitors at all in more than six months, and it'd been far longer than that since she had had a visitor with whom she could exchange thoughts and ideas and feel a common bond in their love of the African wild.

Gradually the sun began to sink lower on the horizon, and the sunset offered a beautiful palate of pastel pinks and blues. Rachel got out her cook stove and heated up some food for their dinner. It was simple stuff, but that's all it needed to be, simple and basic, like everything around them.

Jack got a bottle of wine from his Jeep, and they opened it and drank the wine out of metal cups. This was a rare treat. She had brought a case of wine with her when she came out to the camp, but had finished it all too quickly. When the food was done, they continued drinking until the bottle was empty.

They sat there in silence for some time. Then Rachel felt Jack's hand reaching for hers. It had been a very long time since she had been with a man, and Jack was the right man and this was the right moment.

* * *

She was hardly aware of how they made it to her tent, but seemingly almost instantaneously there they were. She lay naked on the bed while Jack pulled off his shirt and shorts and stood before her. In the low light from the lantern, he was as handsome and as virile-looking as she had hoped.

She reached her arms out and he came to the bed, positioning himself between the legs she had already spread open for him.

He was a wonderful lover, a great lover. They made love over and over, and she cried out loudly in bursts of passion that had been too long denied.

Afterwards, as they lay together in mutual exhaustion, she reached for the cigarettes he had brought and lit one. It was then, as the match illuminated the tent, she noticed the flap of her tent was open, and there were many sets of eyes peering in at them.

She almost leaped out of the bed, but she held herself back. As she looked at the open tent flap some more, she saw the curious eyes belonged to the chimps she loved so much.

She reached over quietly and turned Jack's face to hers. Then she said clearly but softly, "Jack, we have visitors. It's the males from the troop. I think they came to see what the noise was all about. They know me Jack, and I think they're wondering whether you're trying to hurt me. I think the best thing right now would be for you to get up quietly, put on your clothes, and go to your tent. I think once they see I'm okay, everything will be fine. But I think it will be safer if you stay in your tent until morning."

She wasn't sure what to expect on Jack's part, but he seemed to understand her logic and carefully put on his clothes and walked out past the chimps to his own tent.

* * *

Rachel lay there, still naked, feeling the eyes of all the males in the troop upon her. She still felt flush from her passionate lovemaking with Jack. The chimps continued to stare at her.

She stubbed her cigarette out in the ashtray.

Then, slowly, carefully, Rachel sat up and looked around in the now-fading light from the lantern. She needed the suitcase she had brought with her when she first came to this camp many years ago. It was under a bunch of other things but she managed to pull it out without sending anything else flying. She opened the suitcase quietly, and rummaged around inside, searching mainly by feel. Finally, she found what she was looking for and took it out. It was a small round metal container. She pulled off the top part, revealing a somewhat melted but still usable stick of bright red lipstick.

Still sitting there, cross-legged, with her legs open, she took the lipstick and began applying it to her still swollen labia. She saw the male chimps were following her actions intently.

She kept applying the lipstick until her labia were a screaming crimson. Then, closing the lipstick tube, she looked back at the chimps again. Slowly, she turned over on her stomach, and rose on her knees and presented herself to them.

For a moment, the chimps seemed confused and hesitant. Then, Kopu, the alpha male of the troop stepped forward. The brightly-colored backside was a familiar signal, and he was aroused. He quickly entered her and began pumping vigorously, climaxing almost immediately while the others looked on. This, however, was only the beginning. He mounted her again and again, doing his best to completely fill her with his own seed. When Kopu was finally done, Tikra, the next male in the hierarchy took his place. He too, mounted her again and again until he had nothing left. And then it was time for the next male.

Sometimes Rachel would look back to see which male it was who was mounting her, but mostly she was content to just let it keep happening. There were at least a dozen adult males in the troop, and two or three younger males. She didn't know whether the younger males would be included in this. She wasn't bothering to count anyway.

It was nearly dawn when the last of the male chimps finally left. Some had straggled off earlier, but the final five or six departed as a group. The sun was about to come up; Rachel wasn't sure whether the chimps were going to forage for breakfast, or just go somewhere to sleep for a while.

Rachel lay there on her bed, dripping and exhausted. She was still naked, but wearing clothes no longer seemed important. Clothes were the costume and barrier of the observer. Now, for the first time after all these years, she was no longer at a distance, she was one of them.

She thought for a moment about Jack. What had he heard? What did he know?

No matter, she realized. Whatever he knew, or certainly suspected, was too much. He was dangerous.

That part, however, would be easy to fix. After the events of the night, she was their lover, and Jack was a lone male intruder. When he came out again, she would act as if he was hurting her; they would defend her *en masse*, and afterwards the meat would be a welcome treat for the whole troop.

* * *

For Rachel, Africa had always loomed as a mysterious part of her destiny. But she had always been an observer, an outsider. She had been *in* Africa, but she had not *been* Africa. Now she was.

* * *

Rachel lay there for a while, thinking and imagining. Finally, she got up and went outside, still naked. It felt good to be there, in the open, feeling the warm breeze against her entire body.

The sun had not yet appeared, but already its glow was suffusing the entire scene with a warm orange light. Rachel looked around. Jack's tent was still there;

he hadn't started taking it down yet. None of her chimps were up and about. The only sound she heard was the roar of a lion in the distance.

She stood there, taking in everything. Then suddenly she heard a sound from behind Jack's tent—it was Jack's Jeep starting up. And almost immediately the sound of the Jeep starting to move. What? His tent was still there.

She walked, then ran, to see. By the time she got there, Jack had already turned the Jeep around and was driving away at top speed.

He hadn't even bothered to take his tent. He didn't want her to see him sneaking out to the Jeep. He certainly wasn't interested in saying goodbye.

She watched the speeding vehicle and the cloud of dust it raised as the sun began to appear. She couldn't catch him now. And what would she do if she could?

As she looked around, she spotted one of the male chimps—she couldn't tell which one—watching too. She looked at him, but when he noticed, he turned his head quickly, acting as if he hadn't seen her at all. He turned and headed for the trees, and soon was swinging from branch to branch away from her.

Rachel looked around again. Still no sign of any of the other chimps. Everything had gone eerily quiet. She scanned the trees carefully to see if any chimps were visible in the branches but didn't spot anything.

She walked around the clearing a while, trying to recapture the feeling she had had just a short time ago. But suddenly everything had changed all over again.

* * *

Slowly Rachel returned to her tent. Inside, she found her scattered clothes. As she looked down at them, she noticed her legs were now smeared red with the lipstick she had used last night. Suddenly she shuddered at the thought of how she looked. She found a washcloth by her washbasin and quickly wet it and soaped it up. Then, with a slightly panicked intensity, she began to scrub off the lipstick everywhere she could see it. Washing helped, but traces of the stain still remained.

Feeling slightly dizzy, she stood up, put on her shorts, then her shirt, and tucked it in as neatly as she could. She sat back down on the bed and put on her socks and her boots and carefully laced them up.

She sat there blankly for a moment, then got up and went back outside the tent.

Slowly Rachel walked to the center of the clearing and sat down cross-legged. She waited for the chimps to return...

ILEANA

WHEN THE EVENTS I want to tell you about took place, I had been living in New York for just over a year and a half. I was a transplant from the Midwest—Ohio, to be specific. I was working as an actuary for an insurance company and had applied for a position in my company's New York office as a kind of personal dare. I was drawn to the city by its promise of excitement. I also liked the idea of being one of those people who *had what it took to live in New York City.*

My first year there, I lived in Greenwich Village. I was sharing a cramped apartment with a guy who liked parties and having people around way more than I did. But even beyond that, it just seemed busy all the time. There was all this pressure to be hip and to be doing things—to always be "on" as part of the scene. After six months, I was about ready to declare the whole New York thing a failed experiment, fine for others but not for me.

I started looking at ads for other apartments and eventually I found something. It was a one-bedroom apartment in the 30's, on the far West side. Not close enough to the river to have been noticed by developers yet, it was one of those older, slightly shabby buildings where the rent was still lowish. Ten years from now, at most, it would be gone—and so would I. But for now, there was almost a gentility to it.

The block itself was a backwater in time. No rush, no trendiness, no sense of expectations. You could grow old on this street and not feel out of place. After the Village, it was a relief.

The building was only eight stories, with 8-10 apartments per floor. My apartment was on the fifth floor and had a view of the street. I settled in, and then some. I felt like I had found home for the first time in my life. My office was not too far off—a long walk or a short subway ride. And at the end of the day, there I was, back in what? The 50s? Something like that. I felt I could probably have worn a suit and a fedora and fit right in.

I became a creature of comfortable habit. I didn't really know any of my neighbors except for a nodding acquaintance in the elevator or the lobby, but everyone seemed friendly and appeared to appreciate the same things that I had fallen in love with.

There I was, enjoying the best of both worlds—a job in New York, and an apartment and neighborhood that was quiet and safe to come home to. This was an arrangement I could live with.

That is, until my guests dropped in...

* * *

One Saturday morning I slept late, as was the case more often than I like to admit. I was an orderly and conscientious person, but on weekends I was lazy, and rarely had plans.

It was 11:00 by the time I got out of bed, and probably after noon when I headed downstairs to check my mail. I didn't bother to lock my door. It wasn't that kind of place. I headed down the hall to the elevator, still in my bathrobe.

The elevator seemed to be busy that morning, delivering people to floors other than my own, but I was in no hurry. Finally the elevator door opened, I got in, and pushed the ground floor button.

Getting my mail had become my opening act for the weekend, my first—and occasionally only—foray outside my apartment, so I was happy to enjoy it at leisure.

I was checking through my mail as I walked back into my apartment. I had left my shades down but I had left the lights on...or at least that's how I remembered it. Now, when I came back in, the room was dark. I tried switching on the lights.

"I don't think they are working," said a voice.

Someone unexpected in your apartment would freak anyone out. It freaked the shit out of me. My first instinct was to just run out again as fast as I could, but, after all, this was *my* apartment. This was *my* space, goddammit. I went over to one of the lamps, tried the switch. Still nothing. Then I tried the bulb and found it loose. I tightened the bulb and the light went on.

I looked around the room.

There on my sofa was a man sitting, looking very calm. He was wearing a pair of shorts and a Hawaiian-style shirt, although with only a mild gray check pattern. Youngish—mid-30s, early 40s maybe, short haircut—nothing distinctive about his appearance.

He looked like he might be a neighbor from the building, although I hadn't seen him before.

"I hope I didn't scare you," he said. "I knocked and there was no answer. But the door was ajar, so I thought you might be checking your mail or something and I figured I'd just wait."

"Who the fuck *are* you? What the fuck are you *doing* here?"

"Please, can we keep this civil?" he said. "My name is Jared... I wouldn't normally barge in like this, but I've just had a pretty disturbing encounter. Out on the street in front of the building. With a homeless person. I was just looking to talk to someone about it. I don't know if you've been feeling it, but the neighborhood here seems to have been getting worse in the last month or two."

Month or two? Things in the city were always going downhill. Panhandlers, winos, crazy people. That was pretty much a New York thing. Less in the really expensive areas, but basically everywhere. But of course, not on my block. Not before now.

"Anyway, you know how it is. This guy was asking for spare change and I was trying to just pass him by. Only suddenly he moved right in front of me and stood there, blocking my way. 'Spare change, mister,' he said in this kind of surly voice. It wasn't like he was even *asking*. I mean, I didn't want to get into anything, so I reached in my pocket and found a dollar and held it out to him.

"'One dollar?!' He looked at me. Suddenly he was really angry. 'One fucking dollar? What the *fuck* am I going to do with that? Wipe my ass with it? I can't buy a cup of coffee with that. Or anything to eat. *Or* anything to drink. It's bad enough that *you're* walking around, leading this nice, comfy life, and here *I* am, living on the street, homeless for three years now, and then you offer me *this?!*' I was afraid he was going to attack me or something. I mean he wasn't really big or anything, and probably wasn't in good shape, but...you know. You just don't want to get into it. He might have rabies or something.

"Anyhow, I got my wallet and started to give him five bucks. He was still staring at me. 'You son of a bitch', he said, 'You give me *ten* bucks, goddammit! All you want to do is fucking *insult* me! Just because you think you can, just because you think I'm a bum and you're not. I'm really starting to fucking hate you! Give me enough to get drunk on! You *owe* me!'"

"I ended up giving him 20 bucks. He didn't say anything, just let me pass. I haven't felt that relieved in I don't know how long. But, you know, I still felt guilty. How messed up is that?"

He looked at me. "What do you think I should have done?" he asked. "Should I have called the cops?"

"Probably not," I said. "What would they have done? It would have all been just a huge mess."

"I mean, he was right, wasn't he? I mean, in a way. Here I am, warm and comfortable, and he's out on the streets, no place to sleep, no idea of where his next meal is coming from. Why wouldn't he want to just get drunk?" He paused for a moment. "And to be honest, 20 bucks isn't that big a deal. At least not for me or for you, right? So now I'm even starting to feel bad I didn't do more. Like invite him to stay at my place for a night. I mean like you know, let him be comfortable and safe just for one night.

"Look, do you have anything to drink?" he said. "I'm still feeling pretty shaken up."

I asked him if water would be okay.

"Do you have a beer? I know it's early, but after what I've just been through..."

I went to the kitchen and brought him a beer.

"Of course," Jared continued, "you do have to feel sorry for those people—I mean have some kind of sympathy for them. But I never really know what to do. Give them money? Everyone says not to. And then there's no end to it. But you feel bad for them. That's probably why you don't want them anywhere around.

"And now, of course, when the weather is starting to get cold, it gets worse. They're out there all night, while you're warm and comfortable inside, sleeping in a nice bed, having coffee in the morning."

"Or beer," I said, not entirely politely.

"Look Jared, or whoever you are," I said. "I'm sorry about what happened to you, but I have a lot to do today, so I think it's time for you to leave and go back to your apartment."

"I can't leave now," Jared said. "Ileana is still sleeping."

"*What*?!"

"She's in your bedroom. She was in pretty bad shape when I ran into her. Exhausted. Or maybe just drunk. Or both. Anyhow I told her she needed some sleep."

Just then I heard the sound of a toilet flushing.

"It sounds like Ileana is up," I said, hopefully.

"No, that's probably Elmer. Ileana and I met him on the street. He was panhandling. I told him we didn't have any money, but somehow he just ended up tagging along with us. I didn't really have the heart to turn him away. I had told him he could share the bed with Ileana, but no hanky-panky. Not with a woman who is not in any condition to give her consent."

I reached into my pocket and pulled out my cell phone. "It's time for all of you to leave, right now," I said, "or I'm calling the police."

"Cell phones don't work with 911," Jared said, "and you don't have a landline. Besides, Monroe won't appreciate it."

"Monroe?"

"Another one of my little band. I asked him to stay out of sight—until we had reached an understanding.

"Ileana has a drinking issue and Elmer is basically an alcoholic—they're harmless if they're not throwing up or shitting themselves or something. But Monroe is...a lot more edgy. Maybe speed? Or Special K or one of those other new street drugs? Anyway, he's kind of jumpy and irritable. I wasn't sure at all about letting him join us. Frankly, he's a little scary, even to me. But he was pretty insistent."

It was time for this to stop. "I want you out of here. All of you. Now! Or I start screaming for help." I was trying to sound firm, but my voice was coming out squeaky.

"Please," Jared said. "Calm down. This building is pre-war. It may be run-down, but it's solid construction. Not much sound gets out. And if anyone hears you, so what? You think they want to get involved? You don't know them, they don't know you."

"What do you want?" I asked. "I don't have much money, but I'll give you what I have if you leave now."

"Of course you'd love to give us your money," Jared said. "I can see you are a compassionate and generous person. And you'd be ever so happy to see us go. But as you say, you don't have much money on you. And as I mentioned, it's getting cold out. It's pretty nice in here. I mean, where would *you* rather be? Out on the streets? Or in a nice, warm, cozy apartment? We can enjoy the afternoon together, talking about life, watching TV, seeing what you have to cook up for us for dinner. And after that, I think a relaxing night's sleep would do all of us a world of good. Then, when we have all gotten to know each other better, we can talk about our future.

"This sofa, for example, is very comfortable, and if I'm not wrong, it folds out into a bed for guests—such as myself and Monroe."

Jared was looking at the pieces of mail I had put down on the coffee table. "David. Is that right? Or do you go by Dave?"

"'David.' It used to be 'Dave' when I was a kid, and through my first three years of college while I was still living at home. My final year, when I moved on campus, I changed it to 'David.'"

"'Dave' to 'David.' More mature. Not a kid anymore. Good career move. Best of all, it's free. Completely free. That makes it a grand bargain indeed in my mind. Excellent. David it is. David, why don't you just sit down in that armchair while we talk? I'd like us all to be comfortable."

I sat down.

"Monroe? Monroe, why don't you step out and join us?"

I heard a noise in my coat closet. The door opened and a man stepped out. He was black, not terribly tall, probably shorter than me, with frizzy hair—no dreadlocks. He was wearing camouflage gear, probably from a surplus store, and definitely far from new or washed. He didn't say anything, just sat down on the sofa at some distance from Jared and looked at me suspiciously.

"David, this is Monroe," said Jared. "Monroe, this is David. David is our host. So, why don't we all just settle down and enjoy each other's company?"

Monroe and I sat there in extremely uncomfortable silence. Jared found the TV remote and turned on the set. He tuned it in to one of those weekend afternoon talk shows where the guests all try to be witty and chat like they're all great friends. It was pretty excruciating—on TV, and here in the room.

After about an hour of this, even Jared was looking for something else to do.

"David, do you have any take-out menus we might check out? I'm sure you do." He looked around and spotted a stack of paper on a side table. "Ah, here we are." He got up and walked over to the side table and started looking through the various menus in the pile. "Chinese? David, is this place any good? Of course it must be, or you wouldn't bother keeping their menu here. So, Peking Palace it is. Any requests?" Monroe sat there, not saying anything, just looking pissed off and impatient. I didn't say anything either.

Jared remained chipper despite the silence. He pulled out his cell phone and dialed the number. He then began ordering more than enough food for all of us plus two six-packs of beer. "We have all evening," he said. "Might as well enjoy a feast."

When the delivery guy arrived, Jared was waiting for him at the door, obviously not wanting me to have the chance to say or do anything suspicious that might alert him to a problem. Jared pulled out a bunch of cash to pay for the order, and judging by the smile on the delivery guy's face, he must've tipped him generously as well.

I went to the kitchen and got some plates and sil-verware and napkins for us. The pair in the bedroom showed no signs of joining us. "I think," said Jared, "our friends in the other room will probably sleep through." He smiled. "More for us that way."

I sat back down in the armchair and we all filled up our plates from the various containers and grabbed beers to go with the food. Jared had found a channel that was playing reruns of old episodes of "The Big Bang Theory." "See," said Jared. "They all eat Chinese food around the coffee table in the living room, just like us."

I was decidedly not hungry, but at least eating gave me something to do, and maybe if I had a beer or two I might not care quite as much.

We continued to watch reruns on TV for quite a while still with no one saying much of anything at all.

Finally, just about when I was thinking I couldn't stand it anymore, Jared said, "Well David, I think it's probably getting to be time for us to be settling in for the night. I hope you have some extra blankets and pillows for us to use. I don't think we need to bother with sheets. We're very undemanding guests."

Obviously I wasn't in a good mood about any of this, but at least the idea of getting us all ready for bed would offer some respite from just sitting there with these two strangers watching shows I had no interest in.

I didn't want to have to go into the bedroom. For-tunately, I kept some extra blankets and pillows in the hall closet. I found three pillows and three blankets.

Jared had pulled open the sofa bed and took two pillows and two of the blankets. "With Monroe and myself sharing the sofa bed," Jared said, "I'm afraid you yourself will have to be content with sleeping on the floor. At least it's carpeted, and you have a pillow for yourself and a blanket to keep you warm."

Monroe didn't look too happy about any of this, but eventually he got in on one side of the sofa bed, scooting himself as close to the edge of the bed, as far away from Jared as he could.

Jared prepared to get in on his side. "David, I hope you sleep well. I'm sorry we don't have a more comfortable arrangement, but as you know, the host is always eager to make sacrifices for his guests."

He looked at me. "By the way David, I know you wouldn't try anything rash, but Monroe is a very light sleeper and either he or I would be sure to hear it if you were to, well, shall we say, try to leave? I just want to be sure we all understand each other. Get some sleep and we will see each other again in the morning. Good night."

I lay down on the floor with my pillow and blanket and tried to fall asleep. I was pretty exhausted from everything that was going on, so I did finally kind of manage to fall asleep, sort of. I think I spent the night falling in and out of a half-sleep. At times I would hear the bathroom toilet flush, but I didn't know who it was and really didn't want to know. Even though I would have liked to pee, I held it in. I wanted to hide as much as I possibly could.

At some point in the morning I started to wake up. But even as I was beginning to return to consciousness, I remembered I didn't want to wake up at all. So I fought myself back to sleep—or at least something like sleep—for as long as possible. The result was a restless semi-consciousness. I heard the front door open and close. Then after a while I heard two voices, Monroe and Jared, talking. I don't think I had heard Monroe say anything at all before, but now he was talking. Jared seemed not to want to talk about whatever it was. As for me, I just wanted to be asleep.

Eventually I couldn't hold out any longer and had to start waking up. My body was achy from sleeping on the floor—there was a carpet, but it was that cheap, thin kind they use in apartment buildings. I sat up and looked around. I was still in my bathrobe and pajamas from yesterday. Neither Monroe nor Jared was saying anything, they were just sitting there on the sofa, which they had folded back up from its nighttime function as a bed. I heard the toilet flush, and then a white-haired man in completely filthy street clothes looking much the worse for wear came in. I assumed this was Elmer. He sat down in the armchair and joined in the silence.

Jared looked at me sitting on the floor and said, "David, maybe you'd like to go into the bedroom and get some daytime clothes on. Maybe take a shower too. It might help you feel better. Don't worry, Ileana isn't there. She woke up about an hour ago and washed up. I sent her out to get some new clothes. Her old clothes, well let's just say throwing up all over them hadn't done them any good. She'll be back in a bit."

I got up and headed into the bedroom. I went into the bathroom for a desperately overdue pee and took a quick shower, shaved, and combed my hair. Then I went to my chest of drawers and got out a pair of jeans, some underwear and a long-sleeved T-shirt. As I was getting my clothes, however, I noticed everything in the drawer was looking messed up. I'm normally very neat; I fold my clothes, T-shirts, underwear, even my socks, and keep them in careful piles in my drawers. I opened the next drawer down, and saw it was all messed up too. Someone had been rifling through them, looking for whatever they could find. Then suddenly I found myself thinking, "Oh shit!" Being the kind of person I am, I like to be prepared for emergencies, so I like to be sure I have cash around in case there is a power outage and the ATM machines aren't working or whatever. Anyhow, I had put $1,000 in cash into a plain brown envelope beneath some sweaters at the bottom of the bottom drawer. I didn't need to look; I knew it was gone. Goddammit to hell. I also knew there wasn't a damn thing I could do about it. And I wasn't going to give them the satisfaction of complaining, especially not since I knew this was hardly the end of all this shit.

I went back out to the living room. I was in an even fouler mood. I stood there looking at Monroe and Jared on the sofa and Elmer in the armchair. None of them seemed to be paying any attention to me or even to each other.

Suddenly I heard the doorknob of the front door turn and saw a woman walk in. I had never actually seen her before, but I knew it was Ileana.

* * *

She looked...well...stunning. I mean, I was stunned. She had long black hair and blue eyes, and now she was wearing a blue business suit jacket and a matching blue skirt and had on new high heels. She could have walked into any midtown office and looked right at home. And then some.

"So, do I look okay? What do you think?"

Jared said, in a slightly bored way, "You look fine, Ileana. Certainly an improvement over yesterday." He nodded slightly in my direction. "This is David, our host. I don't believe you've met him yet."

Monroe just sat there saying nothing. Elmer didn't say anything either. I think I at least nodded. I wanted to say something, but I didn't. I felt like anything I said would come out wrong.

"I tossed the old clothes in the trash on the way back," she said. "Wasn't worth keeping them in the shape they were in. But I did remember to pick up the other stuff you asked for." She opened a paper bag she had brought with her and pulled out a 40-oz bottle of Colt 45 Malt Liquor for Monroe, and a screw-top bottle of wine for Elmer.

The two men took the bottles and started drinking from them without saying a word.

"David," Ileana said, looking at me, "I need to talk to you for a moment. Can you come into the other room with me?"

The other room, of course, being the bedroom. She led the way in, and once I was inside, she shut the door and turned to me.

"David," she said, "I'd like to explain, at least a little bit, about what was going on with me before. The thing is, I'd gone to a party in the Village with my boyfriend. We were both drinking, and then I saw him starting to hit on this cheap-looking Goth girl. You know, the purple lipstick and green eye shadow and piercings and all that shit. It's all such a fucking cliché. I was looking daggers at them, and I knew he saw me but he was just ignoring me and coming on to her. He's a sleazebag anyway, always has been. I know he cheats on me, but I just keep going back to him. So, what I should have done is just found some guy to hit on and go home with instead. But I had been drinking a lot and somehow I decided to just keep drinking. I guess I blacked out at some point. I mean I was in a whole different neighborhood by the time Jared found me. He told me he'd take care of me and find me a place to get some sleep.

"I guess I should've just gone home, but I couldn't stand the idea of seeing my asshole boyfriend again— or waiting alone all night when he didn't come home.

"Anyhow, I'm really sorry about all this. I'm sorry about taking over your bed uninvited. And I'm sorry about the money too. I figure you know about that now. The thing is, I want to do something to help make up for it, at least a little bit."

She looked at me with those blue eyes of hers, and she did look truly sorry.

She slowly kicked off her high heels and took off her jacket. Underneath, she was wearing a sleeveless white sweater. I looked and saw she wasn't wearing a bra under her sweater. I could see her nipples poking against the fabric.

She kept looking at me the whole time, and I couldn't come up with a word to say.

Then she began to kneel down in front of me. Her eyes were about at the level of my belt now. She unbuckled my belt, unbuttoned my pants, and pulled down my zipper. "I really appreciate your letting me sleep in your bed," she was saying in a low voice.

She started tugging my pants and boxers down until my penis popped out. Ever since seeing her nipples through her sweater I had been turned on.

"Oh David," she said. "Your cock looks so nice."

And with that, she took my penis in her mouth and started sucking on it. I watched her as her head moved back and forth. Her mouth felt warm and wet and velvety, and she kept moving her tongue around as well.

It was wonderful. It felt fantastic. Watching her do it was probably even more fantastic.

Unfortunately, I couldn't make it last. Almost before I knew it, I started coming. I wanted desperately to hold on, but she wasn't helping at all. She kept on sucking and sucking, and I could see she was swallowing at the same time.

By any standards, she was amazing. By any standards, I was not. I was the hopeless adolescent in a 26-year-old body. I was a total failure at this.

Finally she stopped. I had pretty much shrunk back out of her mouth.

She looked up at me. "Was that okay? Did you like that, David?"

Was it okay? The truth is I had no basis for comparison. That's pretty embarrassing.

"It was great," I said. "Thank you." God that was lame, but I mean I was totally out of words at that point.

She stood back up and put on her jacket and high heels while I got my pants back up and my shirt tucked in. "I think we'd better get back out there," she said. "They'll be wondering what we're doing."

I was nervous about coming out of the bedroom with Ileana. I felt like everyone knew what had been going on—as far as I was concerned, they might as well all have been right there watching.

When we walked into the living room, we smelled food. Jared had ordered pizzas and more beer, and he and Monroe were already eating, while Elmer was holding a slice in his hand, nibbling tentatively. "Have a slice, you two, dig in while it's hot," Jared said.

I was grateful for something to do, something to break up the awkwardness of... well, just about everything.

I grabbed two chairs from the dining table for me and Ileana. We each grabbed a slice of pizza and beer and sat down and started eating. Aside from the various sounds of eating, everyone remained silent.

Just as I was grabbing a second slice of pizza, Jared stood up from the sofa and said to Ileana, "I need to talk to you for a moment, my dear."

He then walked over to the bedroom and Ileana followed him. I heard the bedroom door close. I couldn't hear what they were saying; they were both whispering, although whispering quite loudly.

Finally, Jared came out of the bedroom alone and returned to his seat on the sofa. Then, to my surprise, I saw Monroe stand up and walk towards the bedroom. Elmer also stood up and began to follow Monroe to the bedroom. Both men went into the bedroom and I heard the door close behind them. Jared saw me following all this, and said, "David, why don't you sit here on the sofa for now? We can watch some TV together."

Watching TV was about the last thing I wanted to do right then, but I didn't seem to have any choice. Jared found a channel that was playing old episodes of The Three Stooges. He turned the volume up high.

We sat there with the TV going. Jared seemed to have nothing on his mind. I was incredibly nervous and uncomfortable, and obviously wondering what the hell was going on in the other room.

We had been sitting there for a while when suddenly we heard shouting and screaming. Jared rose quickly from the sofa and headed for the bedroom. I sat there for a moment, with no idea of what was happening or what I should do.

Then I got up and went to the bedroom too. When I came into the room, Ileana was lying there on the bed, completely naked. Her body was amazing. I wanted to be able to just stare at her for hours. But when she saw me looking at her, she grabbed the bedsheet and covered herself as fast as she could.

Jared was standing there, Monroe was standing there naked, and Elmer was lying there on the floor, his pants and underwear pulled down to his shoes, and his face covered with blood. I could see blood on Monroe's fist, and blood spattered on the bed sheets. Monroe was screaming at Jared, "I never said this was a three-way, man. I just said he could *watch*. I do *not* share, and especially not with some raggedy-ass old honky wino piece of shit!"

Monroe was pulling his clothes on and heading out of the bedroom. "Fuck this shit, all of you! You're all a bunch of assholes!"

Jared followed him out into the living room and I heard him saying, "Goddammit Monroe. I told you about needing to stay until Monday morning when the banks opened. I made that very goddamn clear. You can't leave now!"

"Can't? Who the fuck are *you* to tell me what I can and can't do? Fuck you, man! Fuck all of you!" And Monroe stormed out of the apartment, slamming the door behind him.

I was still in the bedroom. Elmer was lying there. I had no idea what kind of shape he was in.

Jared came back in looking very angry. "David, could you please go back and wait on the sofa? I'll be out in a moment. I think Ileana would like some privacy while she gets dressed again."

I went back into the living room, sat down on the sofa and waited. Eventually the door opened, and Jared and Ileana came out. Ileana was dressed in her blue suit and white sweater and heels. She didn't look at me, just stood there waiting impatiently at the apartment door.

Jared turned to me and said, "I checked Elmer. He's breathing, he's not dead, so don't worry. As far as I can tell, it looks worse than it actually is. He did lose two teeth, but I imagine they were loose before that. I put them up on your dresser in case you think you want them. You can call an ambulance for him if you wish, but they'll charge you for the ambulance trip and for the emergency room visit. I don't think you want the expense or the hassle. But it's your choice."

He turned to Ileana. "It's time for us to be going."

They walked out, with Jared closing the door behind them. I went over and locked the door, then double-checked to make sure it was actually locked.

I looked out my window down at the street below. Finally, I saw them walking out together, crossing the street. They were holding hands. When they got to the other side of the street, she turned and kissed him— not some passionate kiss, more like the kind of perfunctory peck between a married couple when one or the other heads out to work in the morning. Then they walked off in opposite directions.

I watched a while longer, then sat back down on the sofa. After a while I realized I really had to go back to the bedroom and check on Elmer.

* * *

Elmer was still lying there, although at least Jared had pulled his pants back up. He was awake, but didn't seem interested in moving. I got a washcloth and some warm water and soap and started washing his face.

Once I removed most of the dried blood, he started looking better, but he was in no shape to do much of anything. He wasn't going anywhere today. He kept mumbling he didn't want any doctors or hospitals, he didn't want to end up being locked up somewhere again.

I told him it was okay, I was just going to put him in bed and let him get some sleep. I had a little bit of Scotch left in my liquor cabinet; I poured it in a glass and gave it to him to help him sleep. He downed it in one gulp and almost immediately fell fast asleep.

It was still only afternoon, but I was exhausted. There were two slices of pizza left over from earlier. I reheated them and ate them and finished off a beer.

I lay down on the sofa. Yes, it folded out into a bed, but I wanted nothing to do with where Jared and Monroe had slept. The sofa was fine with me, and lots softer than the floor last night. I grabbed the blanket and the pillow I had used last night, and before I had time to do any more thinking I was fast asleep.

I guess I slept pretty well considering. When I woke up, I could see daylight around the shades. Once again, I really didn't want to wake up; I lay there a while listening to make sure Jared and Monroe hadn't come back somehow. I finally realized there really wasn't anything else to do but get up. I was still wearing my clothes from yesterday, so I was kind of ready for the day.

I went to the bedroom to check on Elmer. He was starting to wake up as well, although he still looked like shit. I didn't really feel like just sending him off looking like that, so I helped him get his clothes off and get into the shower. It was probably his first shower in many months if not longer. I was going to take his clothes to the laundry room on the floor, but they were in miserable shape no matter what. I looked around my bureau and my closet and I managed to find a pair of my old blue jeans, a flannel shirt, some underwear and a decent pair of socks for him to use. We were close enough to the same size, and this would be a major improvement for him. I also found an old coat, an old wool cap, and a spare pair of gloves for him to wear.

At first Elmer didn't want to give up his old, ratty clothes, but when he put on the new clothes and saw how they fit he started getting happier. His hair and his beard were pretty much out of control so I got a pair of scissors and trimmed his beard back and gave him a pretty amateur haircut. I also gave him a paper grocery bag to hold his old clothes so he could take them with him.

I was getting hungry by now. I phoned my office to tell them I was sick and wouldn't be in that day. Then, locking the door carefully behind me (and checking it several times), I took Elmer with me to a deli in the neighborhood for breakfast.

I wasn't sure how used to eating regular food Elmer was these days, but he seemed happy enough to get eggs and bacon and toast, despite his newly missing teeth.

While we were eating, I asked Elmer about the others. He really didn't know much. "I was panhandling on the street when the two of them—that guy Jared, was that his name, and that girl—they came along. I think maybe he was holding her up. At first he was just going to pass me by, but then, for some reason, he invited me to come along with them. He was saying something like 'We're off to see the wizard,' or whatever, almost kind of singing it. He said he had a friend who lived in an apartment near there. I had no idea what the fuck any of that was about. People don't usually invite me to go along with them for anything."

Monroe? "You mean the black guy?" Elmer didn't remember much. "I don't think Jared was looking for him. But there he was on the street, looking kind of freaky and asking for money, and not letting us get by. I couldn't figure out why he wanted anything to do with him. He was a pretty scary dude."

"Then Jared saw this apartment building, you know, the one where you live. There was somebody leaving. He motioned for us to stay back and he held the door for them and then he kept holding it open for us all to go in. There was an elevator, but he made us use the stairway. Finally, he had us wait in the stairwell while he looked around. After a little while he came back and told us he had found his friend and he was going to have us wait out of sight until his friend came back and he had a chance to talk to him. He and the black guy pretty much had to carry the girl. All I know is I must've just passed out once I saw the bed and had a chance to lie down on it."

Elmer looked at me. "He said he knew you from before. Where did you know him from? I couldn't tell what was going on. But hell, I never know what's going on anymore. I have this...you know...drinking thing."

Suddenly he shook his head. "Wait," he said, "me and that girl...yeah...I was...uh...hold on..." I could see him struggling, trying to pull images out of the fog of his mind. "Oh crap, why can't I remember?...I guess I must've blacked out."

He looked at me as if wanting me to give him some kind of confirmation or explanation. I sat there and said nothing.

* * *

When we were leaving the restaurant, I invited him to pick up a couple of sandwiches to take with him. They had premade sandwiches over at the checkout area; looking somewhat anxiously at me to be sure it was okay, Elmer grabbed three sandwiches and put them in the bag with his old clothes. "I have friends," he said quickly as I watched. "They could use some food like this."

As we walked out, Elmer asked where we were. He wanted to get back to the Village. That's where his friends were, he said.

I pointed east and told him to go three blocks, then turn right and keep going till he got there. I also looked in my wallet and pulled out what was left of my cash. A ten, three fives, and three singles. I knew he wanted a drink more than any of the food I had given him, but I didn't want him to start drinking until he got back to the Village. I had no interest in having him get drunk and ending up back at my apartment. I told him the liquor stores around here were a rip-off and he could find booze way cheaper in the Village.

Elmer put the money in his pocket (my pocket) and headed down the street. I don't know if he meant to thank me and forgot, but he didn't say anything more. I watched until I was sure he was far enough away to be really gone.

When I got back to my apartment, I called a locksmith to come over as a rush job and install a new lock. Then I took the sheets and covers and even the pillows off the bed. I took the whole bunch and dumped them down the trash chute. It wasn't just the blood. I knew I couldn't wash any of it away. I did the same with the blanket and pillows Jared and Monroe had used, and Elmer's two missing teeth. I had a feeling I was going to keep sleeping on the top of the sofa for some time to come.

The next morning, Tuesday, I knew I had to go in to work. It took all my willpower to put on office clothes and leave my apartment. I was ultraparanoid. I kept looking back to see if any strange-looking people were going into my building.

By noon, I was a wreck. Instead of eating lunch, I ran back to my apartment to check on it.

It was really hard to keep my mind on my work. My job had been routine and unexciting before, but now it was almost impossible to pay attention to any of it.

I thought about seeing a shrink. But I didn't want to talk about any of it. It would be embarrassing, and what would it change anyway?

* * *

I had always known New York was going to be different—and it was, in spite of my best efforts.

I thought about going back to Ohio. This kind of thing would not happen there. At least I didn't think it would. But I left Ohio because my life was going nowhere. Whatever else, I knew I was *not* going back to Ohio.

As they say, shit happens. And sometimes it happens in piles. As you can imagine, I was having a really hard time trying to focus on anything at all about my work. So I wasn't all that surprised when, after two weeks of this, my boss called me in and fired me. He was apologetic and all, and they gave me two weeks' severance, but fired is fired.

Actually, I don't know whether it was just those last two weeks. I wonder if they didn't find my constant Ohio "niceness" and nerdiness kind of weird and off-putting.

Fortunately, I had saved up some money, so I had a little time to do some job hunting.

I started looking for another apartment—back in the Village. If I was going to be in New York, I was going to be in New York.

I changed my name back to Dave. I didn't want to hear "David" ever again.

I got lucky on the job front almost immediately. I applied for a job in the risk assessment department of one of the big investment banks. The man in charge of the department told me he had a ton of applicants with plenty of experience working for investment banks, but they were always looking for the big score. They always figured they could look past the numbers and find that big hit that everyone else was missing. He didn't need that. He figured that for someone like me, who had been assessing risk for a very conservative insurance company, the numbers were the numbers. I was hired.

And I did find a new apartment. It was in the Village, a rather cramped three-bedroom place with two roommates—one girl and one guy (both straight). The guy had had a girlfriend but they had just broken up, so he was happy to have me to go to bars with him.

Having someone to go to bars and parties with to meet women was a big help. There were plenty of women around, and pretty soon I was a lot less awkward meeting women and having a lot more fun.

In addition, I liked my new job way better. At the insurance company I was dealing with very long-term risks—life expectancies, that kind of stuff—that I would never see the results of. It never seemed to really matter. At the bank, I was dealing with risks that were real time and you could see stuff happening every single day. What I did was actually exciting for a change.

That was two years ago. I've moved again, this time to a place on the East Side in the 40s. I had gotten tired again of the Village and all the phony drama everyone seemed to be into. In my new neighborhood, most of my neighbors are more like the people I work with in my new office. Yes, they care about money, but outside of work they seem more straightforward and are easier to hang out with.

* * *

It's funny. After all this time, I still find myself thinking of Ileana, and her white sweater with her breasts and her nipples. I think of her naked on the bed—I try to wipe that out of my mind, but I keep going back to it. I think of looking down and watching Ileana sucking my cock. I try to stop seeing everything over and over. But at the same time, I don't want to stop.

I don't think at all about Jared, or Monroe, or Elmer. That's just stuff under the bridge.

But Ileana?...

Sweet Dreams, Asshole!

KYLE MURDERED HIS BOSS Sunday night. It was vicious and brutal, with his boss whimpering and crying for mercy even as Kyle continued to pound him with the aluminum baseball bat. There was blood spattered everywhere, including the hallway upstairs and down the entire stairway into the basement. Fortunately, his boss's house was one of those big mansions, with lots of stone muffling the initial screams, and lots of distance between his house and the neighbors.

Finally, his boss had stopped pleading, stopped whimpering, and at last stopped gurgling. He lay there limp and dead, next to the elaborate pool table. Kyle had never been invited over to the house, and had never had a chance to shoot a game of pool with his boss. But none of that mattered now.

Kyle gave the body a kick, not so much out of rage as desultory curiosity. There was no movement. Nothing except silence.

"Sweet dreams, asshole!" Kyle muttered.

For a moment, Kyle felt a rush of satisfaction from a job well done. In the next moment, however, he thought about having to go into work the next day, as if nothing had happened.

His boss would be there, early as usual, and as much of a raving psychopath as ever.

Kyle's visit with Dr. Watkins on Tuesday was going to be complicated.

* * *

On Monday morning, H. Timothy Graydon arrived at his office at 7:15 AM, about 15 minutes earlier than his usual early arrival. Official office hours began at 8 AM, but Graydon liked being the first one there, and having a chance to see for himself what time his various employees arrived.

Marcia, his secretary, arrived at 7:45, knowing Mr. Graydon would have already arrived. She liked having a few extra minutes to get things in order and make sure Mr. Graydon had the papers he needed for the Monday morning staff meeting.

A few other employees came in five or ten minutes early, but most arrived as close to eight as possible.

Kyle Henderson arrived at his desk at 8:08. Graydon made a note of it. Another mark against Kyle. Graydon would be sure to mention it during the meeting.

The meeting started at 8:15 AM sharp, with no excuses permitted. While in some companies, Monday morning staff meetings were a relatively upbeat team get-together to set plans and goals for the week, in this office...let's just say the employees uniformly dreaded it.

* * *

Graydon was by nature in a dyspeptic mood at the Monday morning staff meeting. As always, his bosses at headquarters had been on his case every single day of the past week, setting new quotas and tighter deadlines and frequently sending him emails complaining about his performance, and memos that contained not-so-veiled threats about his job.

Rather than being an opportunity to put work aside and relax for two days, weekends for Graydon meant two days of not being able to yell at his employees and pass along the stress he was under. By Monday morning, Graydon was pretty much ready to explode. It was not surprising, therefore, that Monday morning meetings typically turned into a "kick the dog" session in which he singled out one or more employees for particular evisceration.

This particular Monday morning, Graydon's mood was, if anything, considerably worse. He had slept fitfully last night, and woke up feeling uneasy, though he couldn't say why.

* * *

As the employees entered the conference room, Graydon checked out each one. He could see most of them reflexively cringing even before the meeting began. When Kyle entered, Graydon eyed him carefully. Kyle could usually be counted on to be in pre-cringe mode, and he was one of Graydon's favorite targets at these meetings.

Today, however, something was different. Kyle came in and sat down, completely calm. There was no fear, not even any worry, on his face. He was almost beatifically tranquil. Rather than averting his gaze, Kyle was looking directly at him, almost as if he were observing a lab specimen. This was not good. It upset Graydon's meeting plan. In fact, it unnerved him.

Graydon looked around the table again. He spotted Ed Schultz, who was all but trying to hide directly under the table. Ed was in sales, and it was obvious he must have done something wrong, or not done something he was supposed to have done. Target acquired.

It was a truly terrible hour for Ed, one that would probably scar him for months if not longer. During all of it, Kyle simply watched, seemingly bored.

* * *

For the rest of Monday, Kyle worked at his desk expressionlessly. He wrote emails, filled out paperwork, and all the rest of it. He wasn't bothering to re-check any of it. It was all as good as he had decided it needed to be. Occasionally, he would catch a glimpse of Mr. Graydon, who seemed to be watching him. But Kyle simply ignored all this, and nothing came of it.

Kyle was wondering what he was going to say when he saw Dr. Watkins after work tomorrow.

* * *

The next day, Tuesday, Kyle felt more suffocated than usual having to be in the office all day; it took five o'clock forever to arrive.

He was more than ready when quitting time arrived. At precisely 5:00 PM, in mid-email, Kyle stood up from his desk and headed for the door. He was moving quickly, and managed to beat out practically everyone in the office in making his exit.

Kyle took the elevator down to the ground floor and headed out of the building. His appointment with Dr. Watkins was at 5:30, and his office was a longish walk.

* * *

The building where Dr. Watkins had his office was in a somewhat unlikely location—on W. 36th St. between 10th and 11th Avenues, between the Amtrak and Jersey Transit railroad tracks two blocks south and the Lincoln Tunnel traffic two blocks north. It was an odd sort of no man's land, vaguely sketchy but mainly just an area where no one had any reason to be. The building itself was just as unwelcoming. It was one of those buildings that might have housed a printing plant or something of that sort in the past and had been converted to random office space on the cheap. There was no receptionist for the building, only two elevators and an erratically maintained office directory. Kyle got into the first elevator and pushed the button for the fifth floor.

The fifth floor was as dreary as the entrance, with grey painted walls and carpeting that might've been brown at some point. Even Room 511, where he was to meet with Dr. Watkins, had, beyond the number on the door, no nameplate or identification of any sort.

Kyle had been here twice before for interviews with Dr. Watkins and had never paid much attention to any of this. Now, however, with the events of Sunday night, he was beginning to wonder.

* * *

Kyle had met Dr. Watkins through an ad on Craigslist looking for people to participate in some psychological studies for pay.

It wasn't that Kyle needed the money; it was more just something to do, a break in the really vile rut his life had fallen into.

Kyle had started his job as an assistant manager in the Global Retail and Shipping Company four years ago, with expectations of moving up, and perhaps even seeing a bit of the world. None of that had happened, of course.

What *had* happened was Timothy Graydon. As the vague promises made when he was hired dissipated, Kyle found every part of his personality shriveling, until he had become, like all the other employees in the office, a reflexive cringer whose best hope was that nothing really awful would happen *today*.

* * *

Kyle had told Dr. Watkins all of this at their first meeting. In fact, until meeting with Dr. Watkins, he hadn't even realized how fucked up his life had become and how Graydon had methodically sucked away all his dreams, his hopes, all the promise he used to see in waking up each morning. Lots of people in offices everywhere ended up as drones; this was worse—he was, he realized, basically a zombie.

Dr. Watkins had taken extensive notes. Every time he asked Kyle to talk more about his feelings, Kyle found himself getting madder and madder about his situation.

Dr. Watkins had explained that the company running this study was looking at some potential new therapies for different kinds of issues, and they wanted to be able to understand what options might be most effective in various kinds of situations and circumstances.

* * *

When they had met the following week, Dr. Watkins had put a small plastic bottle on the desk in front of Kyle. Inside was one small gray pill. "Take this one night this weekend, and we'll talk about your reactions when we get together next week."

Kyle looked at the container. He wasn't sure what to think. "What is it? What's in it?" he asked.

"It wouldn't help you if I tried to tell you," Dr. Watkins said. "This is, as we explained in our original announcement, an experimental program. I am working with a company that develops new kinds of therapeutics. This particular program is particularly experimental. We are working with a cutting-edge therapeutics designer, and this pill—REV732 if you really want a name—is one of several new therapies we are testing. Don't worry, it's not some psychedelic from the bark of some unknown tree in the Amazon or anything. It's completely man-made from the base up using the most advanced chemistry in the field. Our hope is this drug will offer people a new kind of way to confront and overcome the stress in their lives."

Dr. Watkins looked at Kyle. "It *is* up to you," he said. "You can decide not to participate and simply walk out the door. But I must say, you do seem to have a lot of stress in your life that seems to be getting in your way."

"I haven't been paid yet," Kyle said.

"We send checks out at the beginning of each month. You will be paid for your time thus far either way."

The bottle stood there on the desk. Kyle looked at it. There was no label of any sort, just that gray pill.

Kyle stood up, picked up the bottle and put it in his pocket.

"I'll think about it," he said.

* * *

Now, this next Tuesday, it was hard to believe all that had been only a week ago. Everything he knew, or thought he knew, had transformed.

Kyle arrived at room 511 at 5:34 PM and knocked. Previously, he would've worried about being late, but today he paid no attention.

For a few moments, nothing happened. There was no sound from the office. Then, abruptly, the door opened and Dr. Watkins ushered him in.

The furniture in the office was strictly utilitarian—a gray metal desk, and two gray metal chairs with cracked green plastic seat cushions. As Kyle sat down in his chair, he looked around the room and realized the office was missing any sort of diplomas or credentials that psychiatrists (or whatever) usually have on the walls to assure their patients of their legitimacy. Yes, Dr. Watkins looked the part, with graying hair and a white mustache that reminded Kyle slightly of the mustache he remembered from photographs of Albert Einstein. But beyond that, his gray suit, dull blue tie, and round wireless glasses gave no hint of any kind of profession or personality.

Kyle was about to ask about the diplomas, but Dr. Watkins started in immediately. "So, what happened? Did anything happen? How are you feeling?"

Kyle had been waiting for the chance to talk about his dream and about what had happened since then, so he forgot about the diplomas and started talking about his experience. He told Dr. Watkins about his dream in as much detail as he could remember. Like most dreams, it was fuzzy in places—in this particular case, Kyle found it hard to recall the beginning. How did it start? How did he get to Graydon's house? How did he even know where it was? For that matter, was it even really Graydon's house at all? And what had started all this?

He had no problem however, remembering beating Graydon to death. As he described the scene, he seemed to relish every detail, and to savor it.

Dr. Watkins sat there, writing in his notepad as fast as he could.

"And how did you feel about all this?" asked Dr. Watkins. "It sounds potentially quite disturbing."

"It felt great," said Kyle happily. "I loved everything about it. I would've loved to have him get back up and beat him to death all over again. My only regret was that this was a dream and I knew it, and I knew he wasn't really dead."

"Is this what you would call 'normal' for you? Did you use to have fights in school? Would you describe yourself as a violent person?" Dr. Watkins asked.

"No. Actually, pretty much the opposite," said Kyle. "In school, I was never particularly athletic, and had no interest in the idea of competitive sports. And later, and in pretty much any kind of situation—from a potential argument with some guy at a party over a girl, to a potential confrontation with a boss—I was the guy who never stood up for himself. So, yeah, this was really different. And it felt really damn good. I mean, why hadn't I been like this all along?"

Kyle paused for a moment, then realized he had more to tell.

"In the dream, at the end, I was afraid that just because it was a dream nothing was going to change in my real life. But somehow things did change, in a big way. The thing is, the deal with my boss has changed completely. In our Monday morning meetings, I was usually one of his favorite targets to go after. Only this time, I just wasn't afraid of him anymore. I had seen the fear in his eyes. I knew what he looked like begging and pleading with me to stop beating him. That was it. And he could tell. He didn't have any power over me anymore. He totally stays out of my way these days. I think he's actually afraid of me."

Dr. Watkins looked at him. "So, what do you think? Do you think this is healthy? You think maybe you've gone a bit over-the-top with this?"

"I've never felt healthier," said Kyle.

"Kyle," said Dr. Watkins, "I'd like to follow up with you on this next week. I'm concerned that if this fades for you, you could find yourself getting quite depressed. Your mood and the way you are describing the situation now seems to be what we would call 'manic'—you can end up feeling very high, and then crash very suddenly and unexpectedly. Between now and next week, I want to give you some pills to help stabilize your mood, and then next week we can see whether any further treatment is in order."

Dr. Watkins produced a plastic container with some small peach-colored pills. "Take one of these each morning, and if you need, you can take another one in the evening. From what I've been seeing here, this is very important." He looked at Kyle and added, "Don't worry, these are nothing new or experimental. They're Alprazolam, trade name Xanax. A standard mild tranquilizer."

Kyle looked at the pills. He stood up, took the container and put it in his pocket. "I'll think about it," he said.

* * *

The next morning, Kyle went to the office feeling full of energy. The work was the same monotonous routine as always, but it just didn't seem to matter. He felt, for the first time in a very long time, that the future *held* something for him. He didn't know what, and it didn't particularly matter. It would happen when it happened.

At lunch, Kyle went out for a walk. He made sure to go someplace out of his routine—a route full of side streets and paths not taken.

After about 20 minutes, he found himself in front of a small store with a sign in the window, "The Baseball Store." The window display consisted of old baseball cards, vintage baseball uniforms, and other baseball paraphernalia. Kyle decided to go inside and take a look.

The store was not simply a collectors' shop; it also sold regular baseball equipment and souvenirs and custom uniforms for local softball teams. Kyle found himself lingering in front of the display of bats. He ended up picking out the aluminum "Babe Ruth Slugger" bat—technically not accurate since aluminum bats weren't invented in the Babe's days, but it was modeled on the size and weight bat the Bambino used when slugging out his awesome home run record. The handle was wrapped in cushiony black tape for a better grip and to handle the vibrations of the bat hitting the ball. As he was taking the bat towards the front counter to pay, Kyle also noticed a Yankees baseball cap. It seemed like a good idea to take that too, to take the edge off—make it look more like a baseball fan thing.

The man at the counter gave him a large plastic bag for his purchases. Kyle wasn't sure he needed it, but as he walked out on the street he realized just carrying a baseball bat while not wearing a baseball uniform would probably look a little...odd.

* * *

Kyle was 38 minutes late getting back from lunch. Normally, that would be grounds for being called into Mr. Graydon's office. Graydon indeed noticed Kyle's late arrival (to the minute), and saw him walking lazily to his cubicle. He also noticed that Kyle was wearing a baseball cap on his head. What the fuck? Graydon decided to wait a bit before checking this out.

After about an hour, Graydon felt it was okay for him to just happen to wander out around the office. He passed by Kyle's cubicle and saw Kyle had removed the baseball cap and put it on the visitor's chair. But he also noticed a large aluminum baseball bat leaning quite visibly in the corner.

Graydon kept walking as if taking a random look around the office in general. But somehow, without even quite realizing it, he found himself passing by Kyle's cubicle again.

Yes, that bat was still there. That damn bat. Why was it bothering him so much? For some reason it seemed very...confrontational? Or was he reading something into this that wasn't there at all?

Graydon eventually got back to his office and sat there with the door closed for the rest of the afternoon.

* * *

The week went quickly for Kyle. And then, for a change, he took full advantage of the weekend.

On Saturday, he wandered around Greenwich Village, checking out vintage shops and thrift shops, looking for nothing in particular. He did, however, spot a secondhand guitar and guitar case. Neither the guitar nor its case were in particularly good shape, but he went ahead and bought them anyway.

He spent much of Sunday afternoon traveling to different parks in the city watching kids and adults playing baseball at the parks' baseball fields.

* * *

On Monday, when Kyle returned to the office (late as usual these days), the people in the office were all talking about the news. Mr. Graydon had called in to say he was taking a personal leave of absence for an unspecified period of time.

Someone from the main office had come in to keep an eye on things, and perhaps to make some changes. No one really knew what was coming up.

Kyle went to his office as usual and did his work as usual. If he was happy about this turn of events, he gave no sign of it.

* * *

The next morning, Tuesday, Kyle came into the office carrying the guitar case. When he left at the end of the day, he took the guitar case with him, and in case anyone happened to notice, the Babe Ruth slugger and the Yankee cap were gone as well.

* * *

Kyle arrived at Dr. Watkins' office at 5:25 PM, guitar case in hand. He had left the office early and made good time. Even though he was early, he went ahead and knocked loudly on the door.

After a moment or two, Dr. Watkins opened the door, looking slightly flustered. "You're early," he said.

"Is that a problem?" asked Kyle.

"No, no. No, it's just earlier than usual, and you seem to be a person of habit."

"Whatever. Look, Dr. Watkins. I've been meaning to ask you this. Why don't you have any diplomas on the wall or anything? Are you really a doctor? What's going on here?"

They were sitting down by now, and Dr. Watkins looked at Kyle across the desk. "Yes, Kyle, as it happens, I am an M.D. and a PhD, and my credentials are extremely impressive. But as I mentioned to you, this is an experimental study, and this is a separate office we set up for this study. I can send you copies of my credentials if you wish."

"No need. I don't really care anymore. But what is this drug? What's it for? Who else has tried it?"

"As I told you Kyle, this is an experimental therapeutic. I wouldn't be allowed to give you any information about anyone else who tried it or about their personal results. I'm here to find out how it works for you."

Dr. Watkins continued, "I spent some time thinking about your case over the weekend, and I'm still wondering about some things. Did you take the tranquilizers I gave you last week?"

"Yes," Kyle lied. "And they did help calm me down. But it was an interesting experience."

"Well, Kyle, let me ask you a question. Given your experience, would you ever want to try this again? Is it something you would recommend to anyone else? To your friends?"

"For myself? I'm not sure. I'd have to think about it. For other people, no way. Definitely not."

Dr. Watkins paused, then continued: "As you can imagine Kyle, this is only the most preliminary phase of investigating this drug. We're trying to understand its effects, and examine its potential value and risks as a therapeutic agent for helping people. I expect my colleagues and I will be discussing your case in considerable detail in making decisions about any potential further steps."

Kyle thought he might be done, but then, almost as an afterthought, Dr. Watkins said, "Also, as a purely hypothetical kind of question, just to understand if there is any potential for abuse here, let's suppose someone got hold of this drug and began manufacturing it on the black market. And let's suppose that let's say someone in your mailroom for example had access and was selling it to people in the office on the hush-

hush. Is that something that you would ever consider buying? And do you think it would be at all popular with other people in your office?"

Kyle looked at Dr. Watkins. He paused, and then answered slowly as if he were deliberating every word. "Would I buy it? As I just told you, too soon to tell. As for other people...yeah...big time... Really big time. There'd be a line around the block."

Kyle looked at Dr. Watkins again, perhaps to gauge his reaction. Then he said, "So, do you have any other questions for me? Did you want to see me next week? And if so, do you have any new 'therapeutics' for me to try?"

"No, no. Nothing else at the moment. You've been very helpful. We'll be in touch if you're open to any further research projects. And I'll be sure your check gets mailed as quickly as possible. By the way, if I may ask, have you taken up guitar?"

"It's a holdover from college. Thought I might try and take it up again. This experiment has been encouraging me to try new things."

* * *

Dr. Watkins waited a full 30 minutes after Kyle left the office. Then he stood up and did a quick scan of the room. He opened the drawers of the desk to make sure he wasn't leaving any samples, or any other traces of his presence. He was a careful man, as someone in his position needed to be.

Watkins was not in fact his name. Nor was the name on the lease connected with him or the company he worked for; rent payments were sent in cash by messenger each month. None of the subjects in his study ever received a business card from him. And, so far, none of them had ever received a check for their participation.

This whole "off the grid" operation was largely secret even within the company. The execs insisted on plausible deniability, and the whole thing was budgeted as "ancillary research" buried deep in the company's accounting.

Precisely because of all this, there were essentially zero expectations about this project. Even Dr. Watkins saw it as a shot in the dark. But now...

This was, no matter how you looked at it, a fucking blockbuster. It was dangerous as hell, but upon learning about it who wouldn't try it? Ideally, they would tweak the molecules to take some of the edges off, but which molecules and how? Everything about REV732 was trouble. Heavily diluted, perhaps it could be mixed with psilocybin or some other kind of drug as a new kind of therapy—maybe a breakthrough in autism or something—but you'd never get this version through any regulatory agency.

On the street, however... *that* was different. All the other drugs—pot, acid, coke, crack, even heroin and OxyContin—were old news by now. This—the "killer dream" drug—would sell itself. The ultimate feral experience, in a pill. Moreover, it was complicated to make—no homebrewers, no trailer park labs. *They* would own it. And they would, at least for a while, keep it scarce and very expensive.

Dr. Watkins locked the office door as he left, and took the elevator down to street level. Then he began walking a rather circuitous route to an unlikely choice of subway station. After about a block, he took the office key out of his pocket and tossed it in a random trashcan. He would have no further use for it, so why keep it?

His route included side streets and alleys, where he would be least visible or noticed. This particular route had become a routine for him, and now, on his last trip from this temporary office, he was not bothering to pay any attention to his surroundings.

* * *

It was as Kyle had anticipated. A man of habit. Kyle had followed Dr. Watkins after last week's meeting, to see where he would go. He had followed him as far as the subway station, but decided it would be too risky to try to follow him down the stairs and onto the train platform. And, as he had kind of realized, he already knew all he needed to know.

Kyle had figured out the ideal place. It was in a long alley, with lots of dumpsters along the way. He made sure to put the guitar case in a clean dry spot out of the way. Then he waited.

Kyle had never really done this before. Or had he? The jury was still out on that one, he supposed. In any case, he was prepared.

* * *

As Dr. Watkins was walking through the alleyway, he was already tearing off his ridiculous fake white mustache. He was ready to be done with this whole charade. Then, seemingly out of nowhere, he saw the dull glint of aluminum heading towards him. The bat hit him on the side of the head, hard enough to keep him from shouting out for help. The second hit knocked him totally unconscious. After that, Kyle was free to pound away at leisure, and he did so enthusiastically. Dr. Watkins' face and head were a bloody pulp, his body was battered, and none of his limbs were even twitching anymore. Kyle stopped long enough to check Dr. Watkins pockets. There were three plastic containers with a few pills in each, and of course, no labels on any of them. There was also Dr. Watkins' notebook with the handwritten notes from his meetings with Kyle. Kyle knew he was going to keep the pills, though he wasn't quite sure how to test them out. As for the notebook, he needed to tear up the contents and scatter them around in a bunch of trash cans in different locations.

The wallet Dr. Watkins had been carrying had no identification, no credit cards, just a bunch of cash. Kyle decided to keep the cash. Why not? He stuffed the pages from the notebook in his pocket.

Giving the body a final kick, Kyle went back and got his guitar case. In it, he had packed some old white towels he had kept from his occasional visits to the gym in college. He also had two bottles of water. He used one to wash off the bat and wash the blood off his own hands, using some of the towels to wipe off any bloodstains from the bat. Then he took the other bottle of water and drank it. All that work had made him thirsty.

Fortunately, there weren't any major visible bloodstains on his clothes, and it was already getting too dark to notice anyway. He put the bloody towels in a black plastic trash bag, and used the remaining towels to wrap the bat so it wouldn't flop around in the guitar case while he was carrying it.

When he reached the end of the alley, Kyle looked around. The street looked empty, so he took a right and started walking. As he went, he tossed the wallet into one of the half-full trash cans on the street.

Then he went to a subway station—not the one he had followed Dr. Watkins to—and took the subway to one of the parks he had visited that had a baseball field. He went to the baseball field, opened the guitar case, and took out the bat. He left the bat lying there in the grass next to the stands. When someone found it, they would think somebody had just forgotten it, and more than likely they would just keep it for themselves and say nothing at all. It certainly didn't look like a murder weapon.

From there, Kyle walked to a different subway station. In the subway station, he dropped the plastic trash bag with the bloodied towels into a trashcan. He tossed the Yankees cap into a different trashcan and the empty water bottles into a third. Then he took a subway back to his own neighborhood. Once he arrived at his local station, he began taking the notebook pages and tearing them up and dropping them into random trash cans. The final batch he tossed into a dumpster behind a local restaurant.

When he got home, he got the guitar and put it into the guitar case. He changed into blue jeans and a sweatshirt and some running shoes, and went back out. There was a park near him where hippies used to like to play guitar and sing homemade songs. Normally he found that whole scene tedious, but right now it was perfect. He went over and left the guitar and guitar case—which he had wiped down for fingerprints back in his apartment—beside one of the park benches, to make it look as if someone had forgotten it. A strictly finders-keepers opportunity.

Then he went back home, and fell into a deep, dreamless, sleep.

* * *

When Kyle came back to the office the next day, he found himself wondering whether he would walk in to find some detectives there waiting to arrest him, or some other signs that he had been *found out.*

There was nothing, of course. Business as usual, minus Mr. Graydon. There was talk that maybe they would have to replace him, and some people were wondering if they might promote somebody from the office to take his place.

Kyle looked at a couple of the tabloids to see if there were any reports about someone having been murdered in an alley, but there was nothing. He thought about checking online, but didn't want to leave any track marks in his computer search history.

In any case, Kyle was sure he didn't even know who it was he killed in the first place. He was certain he was never going to receive any kind of incriminating check for his participation in an off-the-books drug study. No one would ever connect him or Watkins or whoever he was with the anonymous office he went to. It was all a black hole within a black hole within a black hole.

Still, he was feeling good, and he had learned a lot, and Graydon was out of the picture, and wasn't that really the important thing?

THE JUMP

I.

To the Reader:

There has probably not been a day that has gone by in these past few years when I haven't ended up looking out the window of my office and thinking about The Jump and how it has changed my life.

Today, however, I have set myself the task of trying to explain The Jump and how it came to be, and trying to communicate, if I can, whatever meaning it may have. As you will see later, I feel a certain urgency in writing my version of how it all came about. Although I came to The Jump after it had been in operation for some time, I'm the only one who was in a position to meet all the main players and hear their stories, and especially I'm the only one who had a deep personal relationship with Ernst and had some glimpse into his feelings.

Jason Wright
CEO, The Jump

* * *

IT'S STRANGE HOW THINGS WORK OUT sometimes. The man responsible for The Jump, Ernst Adams (he claimed to be related to the Adams family which gave us two US presidents, but he never produced any evidence at all), was basically a low-level con man, always looking for the next get-rich-quick scheme and consequently often on the move.

Ernst was something of a libertarian by nature, though he never really paid attention to political ideas. He just wanted to be able to do whatever he wanted and get away with it without a lot of laws getting in his way.

Ernst may not have been the expert on things that he often claimed to be, but he was very good at gaining people's confidence. In the course of events, he got to know a number of political libertarians, and there was a sense of affinity on both sides.

One of them was Bob Calloway, a half-billionaire who had made a fortune in oil and gas. Bob was especially interested in the issue of assisted suicide. Dr. Kevorkian had put the issue into the headlines, and now assisted suicide laws were being passed in a very limited number of states. Bob's father had died of a very painful form of cancer a few years earlier. He had spent his last few weeks hooked up to tubes and machines, and the doctors had waited until almost the very end before finally putting him on a morphine drip. Of course they had no intention of letting Bob or anyone else hasten his father's death with any kind of intervention.

Bob was deeply angry about this, and the right to die had become his central personal issue. Naturally, he wanted to see right-to-die legislation moved from a state-by-state matter to the national level, but as a libertarian he also felt the whole thing should be a personal decision that people had a right to make for themselves, without laws or doctors. People already did so privately, despite the laws, but he wanted to remove all the shame and all the barriers.

His opportunity came when Congress decided to do a major overhaul of the Affordable Care Act and national healthcare regulations. Ernst suggested to Bob that he hire some lobbyists to help work right-to-die changes into the revisions.

Obviously, this was a very sensitive and difficult project. For one thing, Physician-Assisted Suicide was already under heavy fire from the Catholic Church and many other groups on both the mainstream right and the "slippery slope" left. This would have been a heavy lift under any circumstances. But the whole situation was made even more complicated by the fact that Bob wanted to expand people's right to die to give them the right to commit suicide without medical requirements, doctors, or approvals from medical committees at all. "It's my life, dammit, and I should be able to do whatever I want with it," Bob would tell people.

As Ernst would later point out to people, this was a legitimate claim on a variety of levels. Some doctors, either because of religion or personal scruples, simply would not agree to be part of an assisted suicide.

Furthermore, there are parts of the country where physicians are too few and far between, and it would be hard to justify taking the time to travel to someone's home to administer lethal chemicals. On the other hand, given the right drugs, it's not that complicated, and hardly requires a medical degree.

Part of the idea was that this bill would allow physicians to prescribe overdosable drugs without having to go through endless paperwork, second-guessing by authorities, and picketing by self-righteous protestors. In a less polarized political world, maybe this should not have been much of an issue. But we're not in that world now, and for all I know, we never have been.

It would take an experienced and connected public relations team working with lobbyists who knew legislators, knew their way around the system and, above all, understood stealth. Ernst had dealt with daunting legislative challenges in the past, and knew exactly which firm to turn to for help. They were expensive, but they knew their stuff. When they took your money, it was a matter of professional pride—and brand reputation—to deliver results.

Timing was, as always, the key to success. The lobbying firm wrote up the precise language for the amendment, and the lead legislator, whose campaign fund had just seen a very sizable contribution, snuck it into an obscure section on patients' rights (which the legislators didn't pay much attention to anyway) just before the bill was carted out for a final vote.

The resulting healthcare legislation was as long as a small set of encyclopedias and far less fun to read. It was an ugly pastiche of special interest amendments and rampant giveaways. The process had already taken more than a year and everyone was exhausted. No one wanted to go back to it. And the president, happy to be able to show he was leading the charge on healthcare reform, quickly signed it.

Of course the suicide amendment was discovered, but not as fast as you might think. There were so many battles already raging over other parts of the bill that it was hard to get people to care about something that didn't directly affect profits for doctors, hospitals or drug companies.

* * *

Bob was delighted with his success, and even became a minor celebrity in libertarian circles.

But for Ernst, this was only the beginning of his next grand scheme.

Ernst truly did believe in the right of people to decide their ultimate fate for themselves. But he also felt there should be some sort of an angle here, something he could use. How could he make suicide into something he could package and sell?

Ernst was a methodical thinker, and he set out to research the issue. There were loads of clinical and sociological articles, mostly bemoaning the "epidemic" of suicides among one group or another. Ernst ignored them.

But he did spot one item that caught his attention. It was about a forest named Aokigahara in Japan. Located on the northwestern side of Mount Fuji, about 70 miles from Tokyo, Aokigahara has become famous as "The Suicide Forest." It is indeed a beautiful setting, and attracts loads of ordinary tourists each year. But at the same time, a continuing flow of people go there as an ideal setting to kill themselves. Some simply go there and take pills. More often, however, they use the picturesque tree limbs to hang themselves.

The park was not intended to be used that way, and officials still try to keep people from going there to kill themselves, but it remains an iconic site for people who want to end it all. In fact, a bestselling Japanese book, *The Complete Suicide Manual*, recommended Aokigahara as "the perfect place to die."

Similarly, of course, in this country the Golden Gate Bridge, the Brooklyn Bridge, and other monuments have become iconic sites for people to end it all.

As Ernst thought about all this, he realized there was an opportunity to create a compelling stage for people who wanted to kill themselves.

* * *

Ernst immediately began to think of a whole set of options for people, different ways they could choose to kill themselves.

But he also recognized that, even with the new law allowing suicide, he was treading on very thin ice. He needed to make it absolutely clear people were choosing this of their own free will, and that they always had a chance to change their mind before the final moment.

He decided to create Your Choice, LLC, to provide customized options for potential suicides.

* * *

Ernst's first experiment was what he called "The Thelma and Louise."

A man contacted him and said he wanted to commit suicide but wanted something other than the usual pills or a gun. Ernst searched around and finally found a very scenic cliff. Ernst also found a 1957 Cadillac convertible that was still in decent shape—certainly good enough to drive off a cliff. But, in keeping with his idea of giving the man every opportunity to change his mind, Ernst also bought a parachute for him with a ripcord to release the parachute in midflight if he relented on his decision. Then Ernst hired two camera crews, one to film the takeoff from the top of the cliff, and the other to film the fall and the crash from the bottom.

Everything went according to plan, almost. The parachute was pretty bulky so they had to set the driver's seat way back to make room. Then the man gunned the engine and headed for the cliff as fast as the car would go.

The car headed out into a high and beautiful arc. And *that* was when the man changed his mind and frantically pulled the ripcord. The parachute opened, but the man didn't fly out of the car. He screamed all the way down.

The authorities did not take kindly to Ernst's plan, and the man's estranged wife filed a very nasty lawsuit against him.

Fortunately, however, the crime scene investigators who were called in discovered the problem. It was an old Caddy, but someone had had an aftermarket seatbelt installed, and the man had fastened it. The judge threw out the case in no uncertain terms. "If you're going to drive off a cliff to kill yourself," he said in his rather terse opinion, "why on earth would you fasten your seat belt?"

* * *

Even though he ended up in the clear, this experience had a chastening effect on Ernst. He made money, a fair amount of it, selling ad space on the video of the crash on YouTube but it was clear he needed to be a lot more careful covering his ass in the future. Also, YouTube raised objections to the content and tried to take down his video. Ernst had to hire a lawyer, and they eventually compromised by having him require viewers to certify they were at least 18. He knew it would only get worse in the future.

In any case, Ernst saw that this customized, one-off approach to voluntary suicide didn't make much sense. He would have to spend a lot of time with each person, coming up with something that fit their fantasy, always with the risk that, having spent a lot of money on making complicated arrangements, they would back out at the last moment. And with so many free or nearly free options to kill yourself, there wasn't much room for something that was expensive and complicated and would only end up with the same basic result.

He needed something simple, easy to understand, and that would appeal to audiences no matter what. Something dramatic, something with a strong visual element.

An overdose of drugs is effective, but boring to watch. Basically, you are watching someone fall asleep and not wake up.

Blowing your brains out with a gun? People did that all the time. They didn't need him. And in any case, it was too fast. Boom and it's over. Not really much to watch.

Hanging wasn't much better. Either the person strangled to death (probably not really fun to watch, and in any case seemed to violate the idea of having a last minute opt-out plan), or their neck snapped and their bowels voided and...well, no. Just no.

A guillotine? Definitely up there on the spectacle scale. But who really wants to have their head cut off?

Jumping?... Hmmm...maybe. Definite possibilities. Lots of people choose to jump, often in public areas with lots of spectators. And the spectators seemed riveted by the show as well. Win-win?

Ernst decided he was onto something.

If I may be permitted to reflect a moment, I would say this may be the moment when Ernst began to move from being a con man to becoming what some might think of as a visionary.

Up until now, Ernst had been just going along with all this, hoping for payoffs here and there as he always had. But suddenly, even without having to think it out, he understood his new vision. The Jump.

And once he understood, he knew he could get others to understand too.

The first questions were, where would he get the money to build it, and where would he set it up? He had been spending his YouTube money rather freely on what might be thought of in the old conventional way as wine, women and song—not necessarily in that order—so he would need an outside source of funding.

He couldn't simply buy a downtown building—it would cost too much, and there would doubtless be difficult zoning restrictions.

And finding a suitable cliff in some scenic area would present financial and logistical issues, and would also make it much less convenient for potential spectators.

* * *

Ernst continued to ponder this for several days, until one evening, after a number of drinks, the obvious occurred to him—an amusement park! It was a perfect fit. Even the most elaborate of rollercoaster rides couldn't measure up to watching a real person actually jump to their death.

His task now was to narrow it down to the right site. Disneyland and Disneyworld were out. No, just no. He needed a park that specialized in rides for thrill-seekers and would appreciate the opportunity he was offering.

He began to think about which part of the country to look at. In a general way, the public was becoming increasingly squeamish. The death penalty remained legal in only a handful of states, and in recent years, Texas was the only state that continued to execute prisoners undaunted. Its legislators were adamantly open-carry as far as guns were concerned, and laws and law enforcement were looked upon with suspicion. Texas was, he realized, a death-friendly state.

There were plenty of amusement parks and theme parks in the Lone Star State, but the one that stood out for thrill seekers was G-Force Ultra-Park. G-Force specialized in elaborate and seemingly dangerous rides. Although its designers and engineers were very skilled in making rides that looked insane but were actually relatively safe, even for older kids, the park loved to advertise that all entrants needed to present a photo ID and sign a waiver absolving G-Force of all liability. Millennials loved it; so did hard-core thrill riders from all over the country and even the rest of the world.

The original and mothership location for G-Force was located just outside Fort Worth.

* * *

This would take some serious finesse. Bob Calloway, whose money had gotten the suicide amendment passed, had pretty much moved on to other things, but he still held Ernst in high regard. Bob had a home in Houston as well, so he qualified as Texan, and could speak good ol' boy with the best of them.

Ernst's idea was kind of oddball, but Bob was intrigued by it. It was, after all, his libertarian vision in action.

Bob knew a lot of people, and it didn't take too long for him to set up a private meeting with a few of the folks at G-Force. Bob and Ernst met three top executives for dinner and drinks at the Pappas Brothers Steakhouse in Dallas, an expensive and elegant setting for high rollers and deal-making.

Whatever limitations Ernst may have had in other respects, he was a great and very persuasive talker. Ernst had researched the intense competition in the amusement park industry, and the enormous costs the different parks faced coming up with new, bigger and more thrilling rides to keep up with other parks in Texas and across the country. Here was something that would cost less to build than most of the kiddie rides, and would go absolutely viral in the social media. Moreover, he was willing to give them exclusive rights to The Jump in exchange for his retaining full copyright on all video material produced in conjunction with The Jump itself.

Ernst had taken care to make sure that the guests had all had a few drinks before he began to get into his subject. Even so, the sense of growing shock was palpable. Ernst pointed out that everything about this was 100 percent legal under the revised healthcare act, and assured them that he and Bob would have a team of lawyers oversee every part of their operation. Moreover, The Jump would have a complete option for people to change their minds until the very last minute when they actually jumped. He emphasized that neither he nor anyone else was expecting jumps to be a frequent event. In fact, their rarity would become part of the mystique, and could help drive sales of full-season tickets; after all, the more often someone visited, the greater the likelihood they would happen to be there when a Jump happened.

Two of the men were looking wary but thoughtful as Ernst discussed his idea. The third man, however, was clearly not on board. Almost from the minute Ernst started talking about his plan, the man began standing up. "I've heard enough! I will have *no* part of this!" he declared. The other two men tried to calm him down. "Jim, why don't we just listen to Ernst for a moment? We still have dessert to come, and I know for a fact that this place has some of the finest pecan pie in the whole state."

For a moment, Ernst and Bob thought it might work, but then Jim said, "I will *not* have any part of this! Under *any* circumstances! This is *wrong* in the sight of God! *Goodbye!*" And he turned and walked out.

The other two men stayed put. One of them sighed and said, "Jim's a real good man, and Lord knows I love him, but sometimes he just lacks a sense of proportion. He gets real excitable. Between us, he's sometimes a bit of a naysayer on a lot of the new ride ideas. Now as far as what you're talking about, it is pretty far out, but no harm in us listening to you. And meantime ordering some of that fine pecan pie and another round of drinks."

* * *

It wasn't quick and it wasn't easy—Jim in particular created some very ugly scenes over the idea and finally had to be eased out with a generous retirement package. But with Ernst as champion, it was as inevitable as Texas itself.

Even though Jim had signed a non-disclosure agreement, there was some question about his reliability. Rumors began to emerge, and in these days of Twitter, Facebook and all the rest, the whole story went viral even before the architectural firm had submitted its preliminary design plans.

Ernst began to get a little nervous about the social media storm that emerged. But Tom and Dave, the other two execs at the original steakhouse dinner, remained sanguine.

"Ernst," Tom told him, "this is publicity. We *like* publicity."

And sure enough, attendance at G-Force Forth Worth rose by eight percent that month—and three percent at other G-Force locations around the country. All without so much as a blueprint in hand.

Ernst began to understand just how big a deal this was going to be.

* * *

Things kept moving forward, although more slowly than Ernst was hoping. The architects came up with a tall building with a dark gray stone façade designed to look vaguely like a tower from a medieval castle.

The tower was 60 ft. tall, with an elevator inside, and with a platform about 50 ft. from the ground. All told, it was about the height of a four-story building. (The architect assured them that anything three stories or more would be totally fatal, and said going higher than four stories would remove the intimacy of the experience for the Jumper and for the spectators who would want to be able to see the expression on the Jumper's face.)

At the top was a door that would slide open on both sides, and a path leading out to a flat platform about eight feet long and four feet wide. Beneath was a red-painted concrete circle in the middle of a large area for spectators. The idea was that the platform would reach out far enough to keep the descendant from bumping into the tower on the way down.

It was cheap and simple, but of course there were lots of construction issues and delays along the way, especially with some of the code inspectors eager to do what they could to keep the whole thing from happening.

Eight months later, it was ready, and the spectator plaza was finally opened to visitors.

It was hard to bill it as a Grand Opening, however, since no jumpers had given any sign of interest as yet.

"Don't worry," Ernst said. "It will happen. Just give it time."

* * *

It took two weeks before the first person called to ask about being allowed to jump. Ernst and his lawyers had prepared forms (downloadable from the web) to be signed, absolving Ernst, G-Force, and anyone else from any kind of liability.

Ernst and the lawyers also insisted on a screening interview to weed out potential problems. People with terminal diagnoses, however long their life expectancy, were fine. But he definitely didn't want anyone who wanted to kill themselves because their boyfriend or girlfriend had just dumped them. No one who had just been fired or laid off from their jobs. No one with dependent children, elderly parents, or a current spouse. And no one under at least 40 unless they were terminals.

This first potential Jumper was a terminal. Ed Smith. 46. Leukemia. Prognosis, six months to a year. Divorced ten years, no dependent children.

He had downloaded and signed all the papers and had had them notarized. He said he was ready to go. He was tired of freaking out about his condition. No use wasting any more time.

Ernst and his staff realized they really hadn't planned how to spread the word around the park. The park had film crews on standby and they could be set up in less than 30 minutes. But how could he announce it?

He needn't have worried. His staff had to begin by clearing the drop area of spectators and set up barriers for them to stand behind. That was all it took. The people who were asked to clear the area immediately began calling all their friends in the park, who told everyone around them, and so on. Within 15 minutes the spectator area was mobbed.

Once Ernst was sure the camera crews (one at the top, two more at ground level) were set up and good to go, he was ready to take Ed up in the elevator.

Ed was a little nervous in the elevator, but he was also trying to put a good face on it all.

Then they came to the top and the elevator doors opened. Ernst stepped out with Ed and pointed him to the platform. "There it is," Ernst said. "All you need to do is go out there and jump."

It couldn't be simpler, Ernst thought. Someone who was going to die a very slow and painful death, and the chance to end it with a simple jump.

But... Well, it just didn't happen. Ed started to walk out, took a look down, and totally freaked out.

"No fucking way, man!" he told Ernst. "No fucking way. I can't do it. It's too high. I can't do it." And he started to sob.

Ernst was flustered. What the fuck? What more do you want, man?

Ernst wondered fleetingly if he could just sort of shove Ed off, but that wasn't going to work. For all he knew, Ed would grab on to him and they would both go sailing down.

*   *   *

It was an embarrassing anti-climax, and for the first time Ernst had doubts. So did Tom and Dave. The people who had gathered in hopes of a spectacle were disappointed and furious. Many had given up their spaces near the front of the line for the top rides like Shock Zone, New Texas Gigantor, or Supersonic Alley. They had their cell phones out at the ready to film the event for their friends and to upload to YouTube. If Ed—or even Ernst—had tried to walk through the crowd then, it would have been a disaster.

Tom and Dave had a meeting with Ernst and Bob to discuss The Jump. They had gone along with the idea in spite of all sorts of reasons not to. And now this. And what made Ernst think the next one wouldn't be the same thing all over again? They had a brand reputation to think of.

Ernst asked for a week to think about everything.

After a day or two he began to see what was wrong. Lots of times people who jump from buildings freak out and hang around waiting for someone to talk them out of it. It's not enough to just say, "Here's the high dive, there's the concrete. Go jump." Even terminals don't work that way. And actually jumping? Woah. It's one thing to think about it, but when you're up there looking down, it's way different.

He needed to change the experience. Make it less raw, more glamorous. Better for the Jumper, better for the spectator.

* * *

What Ernst came up with was inspired. He had to keep that element of choice—the absolute opportunity for someone to change their mind until the very last second. But what if that became part of the game? Would they or wouldn't they?

He saw how far he had fallen short of his own standards in his first iteration. Someone walks out on a platform, jumps off, splat, and that's it?

Where's the drama? Where's the something that will make the jumper feel special, feel that they've made the right and only choice coming here? Where's the suspense for the spectators? Where's the play-by-play?

It needed to be a grand—no a royal—runway for the Jumper.

And it needed technology—lots of it. That's what G-Force was all about. High-tech entertainment, high-tech thrills. If people came to observe a jump that was just someone jumping off something, well that just really didn't fit.

Ernst redesigned the whole tower to turn it into a showcase high-tech platform. First, he redid the whole façade to make it much sleeker and more modern looking—out with the medieval, in with the Jetsons. He also added railings on both sides of the walkway—he hadn't originally thought they were necessary, but now he realized that giving Jumpers something to hold on to would help them overcome some of the fear of heights issue.

Second, he extended the platform and had the engineers set up a separate section for the last four feet with a small gate separating the end from the rest of the platform. This last part of the platform was connected to a large hinge and was held up by metal rods.

Finally, and this really showed Ernst's intuitive genius, he would give each Jumper a small electric fob, about the size of one of those electronic car keys, with a single big red button.

When the Jumper had gone out to the final portion of the platform and closed the small gate, they could then press the red button. Pressing the button once would begin the countdown. If they did nothing more, after four seconds the metal rods would pull back automatically and the final end part of the platform would fall back on its hinge, leaving the Jumper to drop. No actual jumping needed.

If, however, and Ernst had always insisted on the idea this was completely by choice and that anyone could back out until the last second—if they changed their mind, all they had to do was push the button again, the metal rods would be deactivated, and the Jumper could turn around and walk out.

To make the situation completely clear to the Jumper, and to the spectators, a large digital screen was set up directly across from the platform, and once the Jumper pressed the button a large countdown would begin—*4, 3, 2, 1!* The spectators, of course, would end up yelling out the numbers the way they do on New Year's Eve at Times Square. No one could ever claim the Jumper misjudged the time.

So, Jump 2.0. Pageantry, high-tech, drama, choice, suspense, even a play-by-play.

Tom and Dave loved it, and gave the immediate go-ahead.

Designing and building the mechanism involved some sophisticated engineering ingenuity, but there was no problem finding companies to bid on the project.

The electronic button fob was actually more complicated because one of the younger staff members pointed out that someone could hack the system and make the platform drop even if the Jumper was trying to stop it. So they had to find a very adept computer security firm to come up with a totally unhackable system.

Perhaps as a result of leaked information, word of the new design soon made its way into the media and went viral in social media. The anti-climax of the first episode was forgotten in the excitement of this completely new version of the park attraction.

With Tom and Dave's full approval, an accelerated construction schedule was approved despite the additional costs.

As a result, it took only three months from design approval to completion. The completion ceremony was scheduled for a weekend in mid-October, usually a time when attendance was slowing because of kids returning to school.

This time, however, not only were they able to schedule a completion day, but a new Jumper had already gotten in touch with Ernst. His name was Bill Stanton. He was 74 and terminal, very much so. Six months, maybe only three, or perhaps even less. Colon cancer. He was already in a lot of pain. His wife had died a decade earlier and he had no kids or other family. He was ready to go, the sooner the better.

* * *

Bill Stanton had never accomplished much in his life. He had finished high school, and then a little over a year of college. He had been a grunt in Vietnam. And then, not much of anything. Low-level jobs working in restaurants or in retail stores. His wife had made a little more than he had, but even with both incomes it was tough.

Now his social security barely covered his rent, and he often missed meals. Medicare helped pay for his doctors and cancer treatment, but even if he had been rich it wouldn't have helped. If it weren't for Oxycontin he would have tried killing himself some time ago. But now even that wasn't enough.

He only wanted two things. The first was the fame of being the first Jumper off the new platform. And the second was he wanted them to put him up in a nice hotel for the night before, and give him a high-class last meal in a fancy restaurant.

This was perfect. Ernst was delighted, and was happy to put him up in any hotel he wanted.

The day before the opening, Ernst arranged to meet Bill at the high-end Four Seasons Hotel in Dallas. He brought one of his cameramen with him to video their discussion.

Ernst had arranged to have a limo get Bill and bring him to the hotel. When Bill arrived and got out of the limo, Ernst was horrified to see that Bill was using a walker. This would not do. Ernst had set up a rule: no wheelchairs, no walkers, not so much as a cane. They had to be able to walk out on their own. Otherwise it would look really awful.

Also, Bill's clothes looked positively ratty. They could easily fix that at one of the shops in the hotel, but the walker was another matter. Ernst warned the cameraman not to shoot any footage that had Bill using a walker.

They went to the hotel restaurant and Ernst ordered an elegant meal for all of them. Bill was delighted. Then, over dinner, Ernst got down to business. "Can you walk on your own? Do you have to have that walker?"

Bill looked a little nervous, but after some prodding he explained that he could walk without it, only not for long distances. Ernst felt somewhat better. He asked about how much Oxycontin Bill was taking. He was worried people might think the drug was keeping Bill from being of sound mind. He had already checked with a doctor, who was experienced in being an expert witness at trials, about how much Oxycontin was too much for legal purposes. The doctor assured him that as long as Bill was able to talk coherently and walk on his own, it was okay.

Bill hadn't downloaded the release forms, but Ernst had copies with him. Bill signed them and Ernst went with him to the hotel services desk and had a clerk notarize them.

After that, Ernst and Bill and the cameraman stopped in at one of the hotel shops and got Bill a brand new outfit to wear. Then they went up to Bill's luxury suite and talked. Bill was delighted at the attention, and the cameraman videoed the discussion to capture Bill's human backstory.

The next day, Ernst went back to the park early but had the cameraman get Bill for breakfast and stay with him to make sure he arrived safely and on time. As part of the redesign they had created a special back entrance for a car to come in, so Bill could come in in his limo through the rear using his walker without being seen.

By noon the spectator section of the Plaza was full. They set up additional viewing screens with video feeds at various other locations throughout the park so no one would miss out. Many of the people in the audience were wearing new "Jump 2.0" T-shirts featuring a picture of the newly redesigned tower. Others had T-shirts showing a picture of the square grey fob with the big red button, and the slogan, "My life, My choice!"

Finally, at 1:00 pm, Ernst went out to a podium set up in front of The Jump and made a brief speech about The Jump and how it stood for the right of each of us to make our own decisions about our own lives without the government or anyone else standing in our way. He then announced that today we had scheduled our first Jumper, a man named Bill Stanton, a Vietnam veteran, a man who has lived a good and honorable life, and who, today, is ready to become the first Jumper.

The crowd cheered, and began chanting, "Bill, Bill, Bill."

Inside the tower, Bill could hear the crowd chanting his name. He was delighted.

The doctor had checked Bill's Oxycontin level and made sure he could walk unassisted. "Once you get up there, you'll have guardrails to hold on to," Ernst reassured Bill.

One of the staff members gave Bill his electronic fob with the red button. Ernst reminded Bill about when to push the button and to focus on the timer screen in front of him rather than looking down.

Ernst rode up in the elevator with Bill, telling him what an honor it was for him to be the first Jumper, and how his name would be in all the papers. Bill smiled.

When they got to the top, the elevator doors opened. Bill instinctively began to reach for the walker but Ernst stopped him and reminded him about walking out on his own. "It's only a foot or two until you can hold onto the guardrails."

Bill managed to make it to the rails on his own, and then was able to make his way slowly out the length of the platform. The crowd cheered.

Out at the end, Bill seemed to be forgetting what to do. Ernst came out and shut the metal gate behind him, and whispered to him, "Press the red button! Don't forget to press the button!"

Bill hesitated for a second, then seemed to remember his instructions. He looked at the fob in his hand and pressed the red button.

The countdown on the screen started: *4...3...2...*, and the crowd was yelling out each number as it appeared.

Bill seemed mesmerized by the numbers, and perhaps confused about where he was. He started to look down again at the fob in his hand. Was he going to press the damn button again?

"*1!*" The crowd roared and the metal rods retracted. Almost instantly the platform dropped out from under Bill, leaving him to fall 50 feet to the concrete landing strip below.

* * *

That night, Bill was the lead story on the evening news on every station in the state, and made the evening news on every station in the country. Bill would have been pleased at his moment of fame. But newscasters and commentators were arguing heatedly over the meaning and the morality of The Jump.

Tom and Dave and Ernst and Bob were smiling from ear to ear. As they raised their glasses in Tom's executive office, Tom announced a toast, "To Bill, may he rest in peace, and to a job well done."

* * *

Although he seemingly had all the details of The Jump itself in place this time, Ernst was concerned about what to do with his video rights. His previous experience made him wary of trusting YouTube or giving it any power over him whatsoever. Instead, he made a deal with G-Force to set up a special portal on its website for Jump videos.

The Jump Channel portal required viewers to certify they were at least 18 years of age, but more importantly, it charged a fee for entry. People could pay for a single day, or they could pay for a subscription with ongoing access to all the videos, past and present, even including the video of the original "Thelma and Louise" car jump. In addition, many people sent in their own cell phone videos and Ernst happily added them to the site. Many of the personal videos featured reaction shots from their friends and people in the crowd when someone jumped. These amateur contributions helped complement the official videos, which focused almost exclusively on the jump itself with only general crowd shots.

Instead of having to rely on advertisers and advertising revenue (some advertisers tended to be skittish about the subject matter), Ernst could now sit back and let fees from eager subscribers roll in. G-Force got a percentage of his revenues for hosting and managing his Jump Channel on their website, but he himself retained the rights to all the video material. It was a win for everyone.

* * *

After that, it was smooth sailing. The publicity brought a small flood of inquiries from would-be Jumpers from all parts of the country. And this was quickly followed by inquiries by people from other parts of the world—especially from Japan.

The sorting and screening process became a bigger deal. A Jump a day, or even more than one, would take away the aura of the event. One or two a month maybe—never more than one a week. People had to apply and be selected.

More men applied than women, so women would get some preference. Foreigners were okay, but no more than five percent of the total. Good backstories became a major plus. Terminals were fine, but not too terminal. Bill would not have made it in this new level of competition.

The last night in a nice hotel made a good angle, so they ended up making a promotional deal with Four Seasons to provide free rooms and meals in exchange for publicity.

In general, the screening worked, and people pushed the red button only once.

But, still, in some cases, even with the crowd cheering for them to die, candidates froze up and pushed the button a second time. They were, as promised, free to turn around, open the gate, and walk back to the elevator.

They became known as "Walkers."

Fortunately, there had been enough real Jumps that these cases were an anomaly, and in fact added to the mystique and the suspense. Once the countdown began, would they go, or would they chicken out?

Radio call-in shows and TV commentators and media bloggers would engage in long discussions about what kind of person was most likely to "walk."

II.

I WAS A WALKER. Or am a Walker. The fact of that moment never really leaves you.

I wasn't a terminal. I may have been out of shape, but I didn't have any medical problems to speak of.

Basically, I was just sick of my life, sick of myself, sick of being a failure.

I was 43 and had absolutely nothing to show for it. My life had amounted to zero. I had never had a romantic relationship. I had slept with a few women many years ago, but none of them ever wanted to see me again. I had graduated from high school and even finished community college, but always with C's and D's, always the bare minimum. My jobs were always dead-end, and I was constantly getting fired. I had no real friends who cared about me. I was, on every level, a loser.

So why not Jump? Have one moment when people would pay attention. One moment when the focus would actually be on me. When people would cheer for me.

I went to the website and downloaded the forms. The first form was the legal waiver, which went on for a few pages of dense legalese but all you had to do was sign at the end and have it notarized. The other, which had been developed in light of the much greater interest generated by Jump 2.0, was an application form, not all that different from college application forms. Part of it was your medical situation—

had you been diagnosed with a life-threatening dis-ease or condition, and if so, what was the prognosis? Since I didn't have any of that I was able to just write N/A and move on. The rest was basically to talk about yourself and your life and why you wanted to Jump.

There really wasn't all that much to say except I was a serial failure at pretty much everything and I was sick and tired of it.

About a week later I got a call from one of the Jump staff. Would I be willing to come in and talk to them in person?

I was living about a two-hour drive from G-Force so I said sure.

They set up an appointment for the following week for me to come in. They had a special parking lot set aside for Jump staff and visitors and I was able to come in through the rear entrance.

They led me to a conference room with a view of the park and all the rides. After a few minutes, a tall, confident-looking man came in and shook my hand. "Hi, I'm Ernst," he said. "I'm in charge of The Jump and I wanted to get a chance to talk to you myself."

* * *

Ernst sat down. "So, Jason, tell me about yourself and why you want to do this."

I told him pretty much the same story I had laid out in my application.

Ernst looked thoughtful. "You know, you're what we tend to call a 'despondent.' Not sick, nothing really wrong, but totally nothing going right. Does that pretty much sum it up?"

I nodded.

Ernst continued. "You see Jason, someone like you is a very interesting case for us. Most of the people who write to us are terminals—people who have been diagnosed with terminal diseases. Right now, we are their way to beat the reaper. I understand that, and I respect it. And they are pretty damn motivated, although we don't accept anyone who is so far along they look really unhealthy—that would screw up the whole effect we're looking for. We want people who are choosing this freely, not gasping and wheezing as they crawl out onto the platform.

"All in all, north of 90 percent of our applications are from terminals. The spectators don't really mind that much—after all, they get to see a pretty damn dramatic spectacle, so who cares about the medical details? But in terms of a storyline, it's not that great. We try to minimize the medical backstory, but the media can see it and it makes us look, well, a little gloomy.

"So when I get an application from someone like you, with no medical issues, just some kind of despair, well, that's a real change of pace. I mean there are a lot of people out there who feel some sense of existential despair, or depression, or just personal failure. And they look at you and they think, 'Man, I can totally identify with that guy.' When you jump, they're all there with you.

"The bottom line is, I'm interested in you for The Jump. The question I have for you is, 'Jason, how serious are you about doing this? Do you really and truly want to do this?'"

That was the most serious question anyone had ever asked me in my life. I had spent my life avoiding serious questions. I was all about just letting things happen.

I looked back at Ernst. "Yeah," I said, "Yeah I do."

* * *

I was scheduled for a Wednesday about a week and a half after my meeting with Ernst. I didn't really have any affairs to put in order, and so I didn't do much thinking about it. Well, I did, of course, but I didn't really know what *to* think. If I had had any friends, I would probably have gone out for drinks with them and ended up getting drunk and feeling sorry for myself. But since I didn't have any friends, that didn't happen.

On Tuesday, I got in my car and drove to the Four Seasons to meet with Ernst and the cameraman. I was looking forward to staying in a fancy hotel, and having a really, really nice dinner. And actually, Ernst was a lot of fun to be with, upbeat and helpful. He got me to tell him about my life while the cameraman videoed us. I didn't end up getting tearful about how fucked up my life had been, I was more like I just didn't know what to think but somehow things seemed to have been on the wrong track, pretty much as part of my DNA.

Ernst was sympathetic. He explained about The Jump, how it worked, the red button, and the countdown screen. And he told me about how this huge crowd of people would be cheering for me the whole time. He talked about some of the other people who had jumped and how they had become part of the whole story of The Jump. It seemed almost like a family.

The next morning, the cameraman and I had the breakfast buffet at the hotel and then got into a limo to take us to the back entrance at G-Force. I wasn't feeling excited, and maybe not even all that nervous. Mainly it all just felt unreal.

Ernst was there to greet me, with a warm smile on his face. Staff members were scurrying about, arranging camera crews and getting ready to have announcements sent out over the park's speaker system. The crowd today was going to be big, Ernst told me.

After that, my memories seem like jumpy flashbacks. I remember riding up in the elevator with Ernst with him reminding me of all the steps in the process.

When the elevator doors opened, Ernst let me go out on my own. "Nothing to worry about, Jason," he assured me. "Just walk out slowly, and when you get to the end, close that little gate behind you. You need to do that for the red button to be able to work. There will be a whole bunch of people down below waiting to see you. Just remember to press the red button once. You'll see the countdown on the screen in front of you. And all the people down there will be counting down for you as well."

"If you change your mind at any time during the countdown," he added, "all you have to do is press the red button again. It's always your own choice. That's what The Jump is all about."

I walked out. The crowd was huge. And noisy. I couldn't really tell what they were yelling. But whatever it was, there I was and they were waiting for me.

I grabbed on to the handrails. I tried not to look down, but I couldn't avoid it completely. I hadn't realized how much I didn't like heights until now.

When I got to the end, there was a small metal gate that I needed to close behind me. Closing the gate completed some kind of circuit that allowed the red button to work. I closed it, and stood there on the end of the platform.

For a moment I almost forgot where I was, up there, hearing all the noise from below, nothing familiar at all. Then, with something of a start, I remembered the red button. I held the fob in my hand and pushed the button.

Immediately I saw a giant "4" light up on the video screen across from me, and I heard the crowd yell, "*Four!*" I went numb. I watched the numbers and heard the crowd, "*Three!... Two!*"

And then suddenly everything stopped. I had pressed the button again. I still don't know quite why. It wasn't really a conscious decision. It felt like nothing at all. But somehow, I finally knew I wasn't ready.

And it had taken this to get there.

When the crowd saw the numbers stop, they went silent. Then I heard them start booing, quietly at first, and then a full-throated chorus of boos and people screaming "Chicken!"

Maybe I was supposed to feel humiliated, but I didn't. I was still alive, and that was better than not being alive.

Holding onto the rails, I turned around, opened the gate, and walked back to the elevator. Ernst was still there, not exactly smiling, but not angry with me either. "It's okay," he told me, "it's okay."

* * *

There wasn't much to do after that. They led me out the back way where the crowd couldn't see me, and the limo took me back to the Four Seasons parking lot where I had left my car.

I went back to my apartment and packed my stuff into my car. I knew I couldn't stick around anymore. My name and face would be all over the news that night and I didn't want to be there for any of it.

I didn't have much money but I had enough to get to California. I drove until I found a little town about 100 miles north of L.A. and got the cheapest motel room I could find. The next day I was able to find a job with a local landscaping firm which had just had some of its employees quit.

This was my new life. I wasn't sure if it was going to be any better than my old one, but here I was. Fortunately, the news about me hadn't gotten this far on the TV networks, and after a little while I just relaxed about pretty much everything. I even began to make a few friends at work, so I had people to have a beer with in the evening.

* * *

I had been out there for about six months when Ernst found me. I don't mean it to sound ominous. He was just curious, and wanted to check in with me and see how I was doing. He had always been friendly with me and I was happy to hear his voice on my phone. His staff had had to do some work to find me, he explained. He had found the same thing with some of the other people who had walked. Many had changed their names. No one seemed to want to stick around in their old life.

Ernst was curious not only about me, but about all of us. He was trying to understand it, and what The Jump meant when you walked. Most of the people really didn't want to talk to Ernst, which he understood. He gave me the names and phone numbers of seven other people I could contact if I wanted to see what was going on with them.

The people whose names he gave me were all living in California, Nevada, or Arizona. I don't know if he just wanted to give me local names or if people just instinctively wanted to head west to start a new life. Anyway, I started calling them and most of them were interested in talking with someone else who had been through that experience.

After about a month, I arranged for a bunch of us to meet in person one weekend at a motel in a small town south of Las Vegas.

There were seven of us in all. Six men and Linda. There weren't many women Jumpers overall, and even fewer who weren't terminals.

We really didn't know what to do with ourselves. Obviously we were very much alive, but we were also deeply embarrassed by that very same fact. How were we supposed to feel? Does "survivor's guilt" apply in a situation like this?

We ended up talking for hours on Friday night, and kept going all day Saturday and Sunday morning until we had to leave.

It was like some strange kind of A.A. or 12-step meeting, only what were we recovering from? But as we talked, I began to realize how happy I was these days, and how grateful I was to be alive. I worked out-doors most of the time, and every morning when I watched the sun rise and felt the warmth of the day, I felt joyful. Most of the others felt the same way. There had been stories of some Walkers who had gone ahead and killed themselves later out of humiliation and embarrassment. But we hadn't. We were alive.

And, maybe for the first time, we had made our own choice to be alive. Before The Jump, it always felt as if life was making all the decisions for me. Now I had pushed that red button a second time, precisely when the crowd below was screaming for me to jump, precisely when I was the only person in the world who wanted me to live.

I could see everyone changing over the course of the weekend. We had arrived wary and nervous, embarrassed to be there—hell, embarrassed even to be alive. Now we were realizing what we had all done—something that most people never do, never have a chance to do, to own our own lives. To take that responsibility, and that freedom.

We decided we all wanted to keep in touch. We exchanged phone numbers and emails and even set up a private Facebook page for our group.

I especially wanted to keep in touch with Linda.

* * *

About a week after our group's get-together, I called Ernst. I told him about what we had talked about, and how all our lives had been so changed by The Jump.

Ernst was fascinated.

A few days later, Ernst called me back. He asked if I would be willing to fly back to G-Force to meet with him. All expenses paid, including the Four Seasons.

I flew into DFW Airport and one of Ernst's staff met me and drove me to the hotel. He signed me in and said Ernst would meet me for dinner.

Ernst arrived at the hotel promptly at 6:00. He seemed genuinely delighted to see me, and I was happy to see him again, especially since this time there was no Jump waiting for me the next morning. But I had no idea why I was here.

"It's good to see you again, Jason," Ernst began. "I know you're wondering about all this, why I wanted to see you after everything that happened. Here's the thing. When I started The Jump, I didn't really know what it was all about. I mean there was all the obvious stuff, and I really did care about people's right to make their own decisions about their own lives. I still do. But The Jump? What the hell did it all mean? Was it just some scam I had come up with? I mean I do have a bit of a history on that score. But somehow, some way, the whole idea of The Jump felt bigger. Only I didn't know how. But now, after talking to you, Jason, I begin to see some of it, maybe. You're the other side of it. But this other side wouldn't be there without the original side, you know? The Jumpers?"

Ernst stopped and looked at me. "Anyway, here's the point," he continued. "I've got plenty of staff. They're smart and they're efficient. A few are MBAs. They do a very good job of whatever I tell them to do. But at the same time, I know none of them actually gets it. None of them *feels* what this is all about. For them, it's another park event, and one that is a park highlight and makes a lot of money. A little bit grisly at times, but whatever. They're professionals.

"The problem for me is, there isn't any sense of connection. Basically, it's me and a bunch of paid employees. But no one who understands or shares my vision. That's why I wanted to bring you here to talk to you. Jason, I want to have someone here who gets it, who can help support the vision and even help me understand it. You're it, Jason. Bob Calloway, who helped me get the whole thing started at the very beginning—he's great, but for him it's just a libertarian thing. Tom and Dave here at the park love it, but they love it for what it does for G-Force.

"I just don't want this to become just another *thing*, another something or other at G-Force. It means something, dammit. And you get that. So, I'm offering you a job, as my second in command here. To help me do right by The Jump. Will you do it?"

That was the second most serious question anyone had ever asked me.

And I said "Yes." I had been happy in my new life in California, but here I was being given another unique chance, an opportunity to make my own active decision about who I was and what I wanted to be.

* * *

That was eight years ago. I haven't regretted anything about my decision. Ernst and I became friends, very good friends. Probably the best friends either of us had ever had.

Both of us were making a lot of money. Ernst still loved women, and the money flowed quickly through his hands, but he also made substantial donations to local schools and universities, art museums, and hospitals. He became a respected member of the Dallas/Fort Worth elite, even though there were still those who looked askance at The Jump itself. In interviews with the media, Ernst managed to sidestep the landmines with his own sincere interest in questions of life and choice.

I too became prosperous, and then wealthy. I made contributions to cultural and educational institutions and to hospitals and medical research. I even made a substantial anonymous contribution to a national suicide prevention hotline center.

I ended up spending way more time than I wanted dealing with accountants and administrative matters. There were constant pressures from the other G-Force parks to expand The Jump to additional locations, but Ernst felt, and I agreed, it needed to remain unique. We didn't want it to become a sideshow.

We didn't mind G-Force selling Jump T-shirts and other souvenirs. But both Ernst and I were appalled when a toy maker came out with a model version of The Jump, complete with an electronic red button and hinged Jump platform and a set of assorted scale model Jumpers. Ernst tried to sue, but G-Force owned the rights to everything but the videos. The model became one of the most-talked about and vilified toys of the Christmas season and was quickly sold out at the park gift shop and in department and toy stores everywhere.

* * *

I still work with Jumpers. For me, it is one of the strangest parts of my job. When Ernst would talk with them, he had never been in their position. I have been and it's a little hard for me to know what to say. I still believe in The Jump, perhaps even more than before, but, well...as they say, it's complicated.

Over time, the percentage of Walkers has risen somewhat, and their stories have become a staple of supermarket magazines. And Walker meetings and groups have become more common. Sometimes I'm even invited to come and speak. I've had lots of publishers try to interest me in writing a book about The Jump, about how my experience has changed my life, all that sort of thing. But I've never wanted to. I'm still trying to figure it out.

Unlike Ernst, I was never a big practitioner of the wine, women and song lifestyle. Instead, about a year and a half after I started the job, I asked Linda, the woman from the original group, to come live with me. She agreed, and she has become my soul mate in life. Ernst liked her too, and invited her to join us as part of the executive team.

* * *

Then, about four years ago, something big happened. Ernst had gone to see his doctor for a routine physical, and the doctor found some problems with his blood test. He ordered more tests, and then some more still. Ernst had advanced liver cancer. It had begun to spread to his other organs.

Ernst didn't mention this to me or to Linda or to anyone. He just kept working, although he seemed to be getting tired more than he used to. He had recently turned 65, so I just saw it as part of his getting older.

He did seem different now, however, when talking with potential Jumpers and when talking about them. There was a new sense of...I don't know if intimacy is the right word, but something like that. He spent more time talking with them, and after a Jump he seemed quieter and more reflective than in the past.

Finally, he had to tell us. His condition was getting worse more rapidly and the doctor was talking about wanting to put him in the hospital. He knew that if he did go into the hospital at this point, he would never get out again. And the pain was getting worse, a lot worse.

He called me and Linda into his office and told us everything. And he told us he had scheduled his own jump for the next day.

Linda and I were devastated. It was too much, too soon, too fast. But there really was no other way. We knew that too.

Ernst hadn't planned to publicize his own Jump, but word leaked out and by evening it was all over the television news.

The next morning G-Force was mobbed. TV crews were everywhere. There was an overflow crowd at the Jump Plaza and TV monitors had to be set up at additional locations all over the park.

That morning was the most difficult of my life. I almost wanted to just stay home, but of course I couldn't.

The staff was able to manage all the details on their own. Ernst arrived by limo and walked slowly into the office. He was wearing his favorite suit. "Well, I guess I'm ready," he said.

Linda and I rode up in the elevator with him. At the top, we hugged him and cried.

"We'll miss you," I said.

"I don't know whether I'll be able to miss you," he said, "but if I can, I surely will. You have both meant so very much to me. I love you both. Thank you for everything."

Linda and I stood there, knowing what came next, not wanting it to, but knowing there was a destiny to all this.

Ernst stepped out onto the platform. "Quite a crowd," he said.

Then he walked out to the end and closed the gate behind him. He had the red button in his hand. He looked out at the huge crowd below and pressed the button. Then, with a final gesture, he threw the electronic fob out into the crowd as the countdown began.

* * *

That evening, Ernst's Jump made the national news, and the video of him tossing his key fob into the crowd was broadcast over and over. Reporters besieged me and Linda for interviews but we were feeling too overwhelmed to talk to any of them.

Ernst's will made generous bequests to numerous charities, as well as to various women he knew. He had lived, as he wrote in a final note, "a life without regrets."

* * *

Ernst left me next in line to succeed him as the head of The Jump.

It has been a profound honor to follow in his path. I have constantly worked to sustain his vision.

I have been writing all this now to put my own affairs in order, and to explain what I can of The Jump.

I went to see my doctor yesterday. He told me my test results—there was, as we both expected, no change, no glimmer of hope.

Six months at the most, probably a lot less. Hard to be exact. But progressive all the while, and moving faster by the day. I have seen the slight but growing tremor in my hands, making my signature less readable. A loss of balance. Not too bad, but disconcerting to have to pay attention at all. Transient flashes of confusion. Am I as sharp as I was? Hard to say, but for sure a few months from now—maybe even just a few weeks from now —I won't be.

By the end I will be weak, confused, and in pain. I may not even know who I am anymore. They would have me hooked up with tubes, and eventually a morphine drip. The doctors and the medical committees will be debating whether I qualify for assisted suicide, have I suffered enough yet?

That is not my path. I choose not.

I have told Linda all this. Last weekend we got married in a private ceremony. We didn't need it for ourselves, but it makes inheritance easier and cheaper. We have been the loves of each other's lives for a long time and I am deeply grateful to The Jump for bringing us together.

Linda would love to have me wait, probably to wait until it was too late. But she understands. Leaving her is my only regret.

Tomorrow morning, I will return to The Jump, but this time for the last time. I will press the button only once. Then, in accord with the example set by Ernst, I will throw the fob out, into the crowd below. Four seconds later, the platform will drop out from under me.

It will, whatever else, be quick. And it will be, as it should be, my own personal decision about my life.

There will be spectators, probably a great many. Some, as always, just for the spectacle. Others— friends, some fellow Walkers—will be there as sympathetic witnesses.

I go knowing that Linda is here to continue what we have begun. And since Ernst's Jump, we have brought in new people as well—all Walkers themselves—who understand and share our commitment to preserving the ways and traditions of The Jump.

* * *

What is the meaning of The Jump? I can't tell you. I've never been one with words. I can only say I *feel* it. It changed everything for me.

Did Ernst know? One night over drinks by the pool at his house, we were looking up at the Milky Way. After a while Ernst said, almost in a whisper, maybe to me, maybe to himself, "On The Jump, you have four seconds to decide. There is no compromise, only decision. You are the *only* one with the power. What anyone else thinks doesn't matter. What *everyone* else thinks doesn't matter. For those four seconds, you hold the universe in your hands. *That* is the lesson of The Jump."

II.

BONUS TRACKS

SCHRODINGER'S GIRL

THERE WAS A GIRL. An average sort of girl. Not an average girl exactly. But average in the way that you wouldn't notice her, wouldn't remember her. On the street, your gaze wouldn't follow her—there would be other girls, prettier girls, sexier girls, even uglier girls, to notice.

You wouldn't remember her from high school. If she was in a class with you, it would be as if her seat was somehow unoccupied. If she was in an office where you worked and she left, no one would ever say, some time later, "Hey, do you remember so and so?" No one would ever add, "Oh yeah, remember the time she did such and such?" She was like Schrödinger's cat—she existed and did not exist at the same time.

Her name was...well, actually I've forgotten. We'll have to make up a name for her. Is Rebecca okay? Or maybe Jane? Okay, Rebecca Jane it is. We can call her RJ for short, although that might make her memorable in a way that she never was.

Look, I know you still don't remember her. Even now, with all my prompting. But she was always there. For you, she was like wallpaper. Old wallpaper, with no color or design worth noticing.

Today, however, that's a problem. Because she always noticed you. And she wanted you to notice her. She wanted that very much.

And when you didn't notice her, RJ was disappointed. Then *very* disappointed. But she was also very shy, and couldn't bring herself to talk to you.

And so she waited.

And after high school, she went to State, same as you. She had good grades and had other choices, but she wanted to be where you were. She took as many classes with you as she could. And you still didn't notice.

In college, you liked parties. She was too shy to go to parties. So no chance of a drunken one-night hookup. Who knows? It might have made all the difference.

After college, you went to work at a big accounting firm. She got a job at the same firm. You got an office. She got a desk out there with all the other drones. She saw you come in every morning. You never saw her at all.

So, fast forward five years. You got married last year. To your hot secretary. Kid on the way. Life is good.

But for RJ? Hell, let's just drop this whole "RJ" thing and use her real name—Emily. Emily? You remember now? Does that help, at all? I know, I know— of course not.

It's Emily's five-year anniversary at the firm. She started a week after you. A week ago, the other guys took you out for drinks. Today, Emily is as unnoticed by the people around her as she is by you. Just another day of existing/not existing.

Something has been building up in Emily. All these years. If you, or even someone else, had done something, anything, in all these long years, today might be different. But that never happened.

In college, Emily didn't just take accounting. She also took chemistry, and advanced chemistry. And despite her wallpaper demeanor, she learned some badass stuff. Poisons. Explosives. Acids that eat through anything.

She was also in the gun club. You didn't know that, did you? Of course not. But she practiced with .38s, Glocks, Lugers, shotguns, and even sniper rifles. She never entered any competitions, but she was good. *Very* good.

So, I'm worried a bit. About you. And about Emily. Four years in the same high school. Four years in the same college. Five years in the same office. You never *noticed*?

Look. I'm thinking this week is it. Either it happens, or it passes. But as for me, if I were you, I'd be really careful this week. *Really* careful.

Fast, Faster, Fastest

May 6

My new handle: *Dude@fastathon*™ Totally digging it. #lookgood/feelgood/dogood

May 6

Going to register this morning. Big day. Am I ready? Month to prepare. #gettingready

May 6

Check website. Fast-Faster-Fastest. FasttoFightObesity.org. Register online. Better than signing up in public. My own personal commitment. #fasttofightobesity

May 6

Fast=6 hrs. Faster=9 hrs. Fastest=12 hrs. Not going to wimp out now. Full-on. Fastest. $100. #fasttofightobesity #fastest

May 6

Texted me my registration number. Number 33. Very cool. Prime number. Number to watch. Watch me go! #fasttofightobesity #fastest

May 6

Haven't told anyone in the office about it. Want to keep it private. Tired of jokes about my weight. #noweightshame

May 8

Three other people in office have signed up. 1 Fast, 2 Faster. Look at me to see if I will say anything. My secret. #pissedoff

May 8

Starting to train. Waiting full 3 hours between breakfast and lunch. #fasttofightobesity #intraining

May 11

Training 3 days already. Feeling good. Sun up earlier. All is bright. #fasttofightobesity #goodjob

May 13

Upping training. Now fasting 3 hrs between lunch and dinner too. Total = 6 hrs fasting a day. #fasttofightobesity #gettingserious

May 14

Did it! Suggested reading: *Hunger Artist* by Franz Kafka. Inspiring. If he can do it, I can too. #fasttofightobesity #kafka-hungerartist #waytogo

May 16

New challenge. Up fasting to 4 hrs from breakfast to lunch. #fasttofightobesity #extradonutforbreakfast

May 16

Change in plan. Fast 3½ hrs from breakfast to lunch. Can't push lunch-hour too late in office. Wait for weekend. #fasttofightobesity #learningtopacemyself

May 16

Extra complication. Wife doesn't want to change dinner-time. Kids hungry. Haven't told them my plan. #fasttofightobesity #familyproblems

May 16

This is day 10. 3 wks to go. Feeling the urgency. Drank extra cup of coffee to help me last till lunch. Got shaky, had to eat 2nd donut. #fasttofightobesity #learningtofight

May 17

Read fat controls hunger longer. Bagel with cream cheese for breakfast. Chose fat-free because low-cal. Didn't help. #fasttofightobesity #gettinghungry

May 18

Starting to hit national news. 1st Annual Fastathon. Like this more as community event. #fasttofightobesity #keepitsimple

May 19

Looks like network news crews and reporters will cover. WTF? Go away. #fasttofightobesity #keepitsimple

May 20

Googling fasting. After 6 hrs, ketosis sets in. Hope doesn't hurt too much. #fasttofightobesity #getting-nervous

May 20

25 % of food energy goes to brain. Will try not to think very much. #fasttofightobesity #keepitsimple

May 21

Just over 2 wks to go. Feeling the urgency. Need to go to the mall to buy clothes for event. #fasttofightobesity #feelingtheurgency

May 22

At mall this morning. New running shoes, cargo shorts, running jacket. Ordered event T-shirt online. Rockin' the style. #fasttofightobesity #dressforsuccess

May 22

Breakfast at McDonald's at the mall this morning. Skipping lunch. Time to get in a full 6-hr fast before dinner. #fasttofightobesity #intraining #gettingserious

May 22

Almost made it. 5½ hrs. Wife making tacos for dinner. Had out chips and fresh guac. My weak. But still... good job. Halfway there. #fasttofightobesity #intraining #gettingserious #tacos

May 23

Fasting getting me more connected spiritually. Almost went to church but watched golf on TV instead. Greens make me think of nature. #fasttofightobesity #gettingspiritual

May 24

Back to work. Hangover. Nuff said. 2 wks left. Ready to get serious again. Just one donut for breakfast, 3 hrs till lunch. #fasttofightobesity #lapsesarehuman

May 25

Back on track. Double-burger for lunch, feel better. Will wait the full 3 hrs till dinner. #fasttofightobesity #intraining #gettingserious

May 26

Think people in the office are noticing. Weight the same, maybe just more confident about myself. Definitely on the right track. #fasttofightobesity #intraining #gettingserious

May 27

Feel like whole new life starting. Hear birds chirping in the morning. Life has a new sense of purpose. #fasttofightobesity #focus #gettingspiritual

May 28

Checked the website. Over 300 people so far. Only 50 doing the Fastest. Trying to be like no big deal, but inside feeling a little special. #fasttofightobesity #fastest #proud

May 29

New development. Added new category—the mini-fast. Just 3 hrs. (for $25) This is wrong. Any idiot can do 3 hrs. #fasttofightobesity #pissedoff #settingthebartoolow

May 29

Still pissed about mini-fast. Makes me want to go out and binge-eat. Maybe I will. #fasttofightobesity #pissedoff #settingthebartoolow

May 29

Bad idea. Not used to so much food anymore. Should have stopped at 1 large pizza. #feelinguilty #feelingbad

May 30

Shit. One week to go. No more setbacks. Only food and water this whole week. #fasttofightobesity #gettingbackontrack

May 31

Back in office. Regular schedule. Last week. On track. Discipline. #fasttofightobesity #gettingbackontrack

June 1

Woman in office saying FTFO is stupid. If you haven't tried it, of course you don't get it. #fasttofightobesity #goodcause

June 2

3 straight days of 2 3-hr fasts. Getting there fast. (My bad.) #fasttofightobesity

June 3

Told my wife & kids last nite about being in FTFO. They all thought it sounded dumb. No respect. #fasttofightobesity #goodcause

June 4

Drove by high school athletic fields last night after work. Track, bleachers, baseball diamond. Hope for good weather. Getting excited. #fasttofightobesity #goodcause

June 5

Saturday. Tomorrow's the day. T-shirt came in the mail yesterday. Can't wait. #fasttofightobesity #excited

June 6

Woke up early. Sun's up. Beautiful morning. Fasting-prep breakfast—eggs & extra bacon, 4 slices of toast, orange juice. Ready. #fasttofightobesity #excited

June 6

Wife & kids not coming. Maybe later. Arrived early. First food trucks already in place outside the fence. Smelling the bacon cooking. #fasttofightobesity #bacon

June 6

Quick breakfast sandwich—double egg, double bacon, no cheese. Mmmm. Will last me a long time. Has to. #fasttofightobesity #goodfood

June 6

Signed in at 8:50, ten minutes before the deadline. Brought reclining lawn chair with me—bleachers would be killing my back. #fasttofightobesity #comfort

June 6

1st news crews showing up. Film some people signing in, do a few interviews, get bored, stand around. #fasttofightobesity

June 6

Tent near entrance set up for medical crew. One volunteer nurse is there so far. No sign of medical emergencies yet. #fasttofightobesity

June 6

Lots of extra people showing up at the last minute wanting to sign up. They're letting them. Guess it's for the money. Not fair. #fasttofightobesity #rulesaremade

June 6

We all have our numbers pinned on, also have FTFO caps to indicate which fast we're doing. Fast – yellow. Faster – blue. Fastest – red. #fasttofightobesity #redcappride

June 6

The minis have white caps. I don't even want to look at them. #fasttofightobesity #redcappride

June 6

More food trucks showing up. Pizza, burgers, gyros, tacos, BBQ, Nicaraguan food (WTF?). Maybe a salad bar, but who cares? #fasttofightobesity #goodfood

June 6

Spotted some people from work, but have tried to duck out of sight. Saw some other people I know with red caps. Will talk to them. #fasttofightobesity #sociable

June 6

A few spectators have arrived, not many. Not much to watch yet. Probably some of the white caps have people coming to meet them for lunch. #fasttofightobesity #passingtime

June 6

11:20 am. I see some white caps already checking the food trucks to see what they want for lunch. Why are they even here? #fasttofightobesity #pissedoff

June 6

12:00 pm. White caps are heading for the exit. Some not even signing out. As I say, why bother? Good riddance. #fasttofightobesity #whitecapsbad

June 6

1:00 pm. Now that the white caps and their buddies are gone, it's starting to feel like a real fast. Good. I'm ready. #fasttofightobesity

June 6

Some people are starting to walk around the track in groups. Not sure if they're showing off or just bored. #fasttofightobesity

June 6

2:30. See some of the yellow caps looking over to check out the food stands. Wonder if they'll make it to 3:00? #fasttofightobesity #hangingin

June 6

3:00 Remaining yellow caps heading out. A few spectators applauding them. Really? TV crews start interviewing. #fasttofightobesity

June 6

3:15. Starting to get antsy. Definitely feeling the hunger. Will find some other red caps to walk the track with. #fasttofightobesity

June 6

3:30. Found 4 other red caps. I'm going to go out fast, show everyone. Liking my new duds. #fasttofightobesity

June 6

3:40. Started out fast, left others behind. By halfway mark, got winded. Have to stop. Will let others catch up. Polite thing to do. #fasttofightobesity #learningtopacemyself

June 6

3:50. Let others catch up. Decided to stop at ¾ mark. That's most of a quarter-mile. Need more practice. #fasttofightobesity #learningtopacemyself

June 6

There's bottled water on ice for us everywhere. Important to stay hydrated. #fasttofightobesity #gettingtiredofwater

June 6

Went over to talk to some of the red caps I was walking with. They seem kind of huffy to me. Don't know why. But I'm good. #fasttofightobesity #doingitonmyown

June 6

It's after 5 now. I can see some of the blue caps are checking out the food trucks. I'm hungry too, but so what? I can hold out. #fasttofightobesity #kafka-hungerartist #waytogo

June 6

5:55. Blue caps are lining up to sign out. Families are joining them. More spectators now, more applause. Some standing applause. #fasttofightobesity

June 6

Two ambulances have arrived and parked outside the fence. No emergency for now. Good to be prepared. #fasttofightobesity

June 6

TV crews having a field day with blue cap interviews. Like it's some sort of big deal. Not so much. #fasttofightobesity

June 6

Some red cap brought a portable TV and is watching Big Bang Theory. Asshole. This is supposed to be a fast. Not just a regular day. #fasttofightobesity #doitright

June 6

7:00 pm. Hungry. Really, really hungry. Is this what ketosis feels like? It can't be healthy to be in this much pain. #fasttofightobesity #ketosis

June 6

One hour and 45 minutes to go. Feeling giddy. Wish family would show up. #fasttofightobesity #lonelinessofthelongdistancefaster

June 6

Wondering if I should go to the medical tent. Just to be sure. Decide to adjust the back of my chair a notch. More restful. #fasttofightobesity #beingcareful

June 6

8:00. One hour to go. More spectators arrive. Mostly family members. I'm still on my own. Sure wife & kids had dinner without me. #fasttofightobesity #pissedoff

June 6

8:15. Looks like some of the food trucks are shutting down. Hope they don't *all* leave. Have been carrying $30 in cash for food. #fasttofightobesity #reallyhungry

June 6

8:30. More food trucks closing down. Can't quit now, can I? Damn. #fasttofightobesity #quandry

June 6

See the TV crews packing up and leaving. They're not going to interview *us*? What the fuck? So wrong. #fasttofightobesity #pissedoff

June 6

8:45. Red caps starting to make their way to the sign-out table. Feeling weak. Can I carry my chair, or should I drag it? #fasttofightobesity #needingmedicalattention

June 6

9:05. Still waiting in line to sign out. Too slow. Hardly any spectators left, just family. Where's the applause? No food trucks left. #fasttofightobesity #pissedoff

June 6

9:15. Good news! Red caps get gift bags for going the distance. Assortment of candy bars. Best Snickers ever! Saving M&Ms for dessert. #fasttofightobesity #blessed

June 7

Back in office. Checking website. Big success. Want suggestions for next year. Mine: Ultra-fast: 15 hrs. Full year to get ready. #fasttofightobesity #gettingready

THE BARBIE MASSACRE

LIANA WILLIAMS WAS A COUNSELOR at a local junior high school. She spent her days talking to students dealing with the many traumas of budding adolescence, childhood and family issues (including poverty), and the challenges of preparing for adulthood. All too often, the job left her exhausted and emotionally drained.

Her current challenge was trying to help Sofia, an eighth-grader who had come to Brooklyn from Puerto Rico. Sofia was an average-looking girl with a nice smile and friendly personality. Despite her best efforts to fit in and make friends, she found herself an outcast. She was not technically an immigrant, but found herself isolated from the Anglo girls, who didn't want her hanging out with them, and from the Hispanic students from different Latin and South American countries, who also didn't accept her as one of them.

Sofia had recently become a target for cyber bullying by some of the girls who would use Instagram to post pictures of her from awkward angles and in the most unflattering situations with humiliating captions.

This was a sweet girl who was trying hard and had lots to offer, and she had run into the brick wall of teenage culture and behavior. But she was only one of the dozens of students Liana was trying to help. And she knew nothing she could do would be enough to really help any of them, let alone all of them.

Dealing with young girls who would come crying into her office with tales of online bullying had made Liana more and more acutely aware of the disastrous impact of popular culture and social media on the self-image of vulnerable adolescents. And reading the news in the papers and online about the #MeToo movement and the way women had been treated all this time sickened her.

She was determined to do whatever she could to stop the madness.

* * *

Being a school counselor was Liana's "job" job. Her other job was being a mom. She was divorced from her husband and was the primary custodial parent of Tammi, who was about to turn eight years old.

Liana loved Tammi. Of course she did. That was a given, that was a mother's job. But she was a lot less sure she actually *liked* Tammi. It was pretty clear, even to her, that she wasn't instinctively *proud* of Tammi. When she was around other mothers and their daughters—daughters who were smart and energetic and undeniably attractive—it was hard for her to tell herself she was happy that *her* daughter was Tammi.

Liana was moderately athletic by nature, and had been so since childhood. She still jogged, though more intermittently than in the past. And, as is so often the case when one edges past 30, she had added a number of pounds around her legs and middle. Even so, she was in better shape than most of the women she knew.

Tammi, however, was different. There was nothing naturally athletic about her. She was heavy and clumsy and, sad to say, whiny. Already her knees splayed inward, so neither track nor jogging lay in her future. Academically, she was in the low middle, not something to despair about, but given the career focus of both her parents, definitely a disappointment.

Liana wondered how she would feel if one of the other mothers was Tammi's mother. She suspected she would feel grateful that Tammi was not *her* daughter. The truth of this thought made her feel guilty, and made her feel absolutely determined to do right by Tammi no matter what.

* * *

Doing right, of course, was a tricky business. Tammi loved Froot Loops, that dreadful sugar-laden breakfast concoction that cynical marketers spent millions of dollars advertising to kids. When Liana tried to steer Tammi to something like oatmeal or even bacon and eggs and toast, Tammi would whine like crazy. Still, Liana persisted in what she knew was best for Tammi. She knew that on the alternate weekends that Tammi spent with her father, he would indulge her with Froot Loops and junk food and reactivate her expectation that she should be treated like a normal American Froot Loops-eating child.

The divorce had not been pleasant—even civil would be a bit of a stretch. Her ex-husband's incessant description of her as a "controlling bitch" infuriated her, but all she could think of to call him was "asshole." It was easy to understand why divorced dads would indulge their kids in the time they had with them and thereby curry their favor, but Liana resented the hell out of being stuck with being "the sensible one." And she was by no means sure Tammi would ever look back and thank her for all that she had done. Her faith in Tammi's common sense and understanding was limited to say the least.

* * *

Tammi's eighth birthday was coming up in a few weeks. Naturally, she was excited and had already assembled a list of presents she wanted/expected. And at the top of the list was a Barbie doll. All her friends— her friends being the two other girls who lived on her block and were more or less stuck with including her in their circle, though they would doubtless leave her behind when they got old enough to visit other friends on other blocks on their own—*all* her friends had Barbies. Of course Tammi wanted a Barbie. She wanted to be able to join her friends in their Barbie parties and Barbie play. Why couldn't Liana just accept that and go with it?

But of course, she couldn't. She knew about Barbie's sordid history, modeled on a German porn doll. But most important, she was acutely aware of the threat the big boobed, slim waisted, and long-legged doll posed to the body image of young girls who could never live up to this plastic ideal in their own lives.

Liana *hated* the idea of buying Tammi a Barbie. But she knew full well Tammi's father would buy her half a dozen Barbies just to piss her mom off. So she very reluctantly began to research her options.

She was pleased to discover that many other moms had the same concern she had, and that the extent of the public outcry on this issue had finally forced Mattel to come up with some alternatives. Barbies now came in a variety of skin colors, and even offered a new choice of shapes—in particular, Curvy Barbie, shorter than the original Barbie, with smaller breasts and hippier hips. Here was a doll with more *realistic* proportions, a doll that would not instill its young owner with dysmorphic shame.

* * *

Now Liana had a plan, something that would work for both her and her daughter. She told Tammi the two of them would go out shopping together that weekend.

The toy store they went to was located in a nearby indoor mini-mall. The store was compact but well-stocked, and had a full selection of Barbies, Bratz, and other popular doll brands. Liana had even called the store ahead of time to be sure they had Curvy Barbies in stock.

Tammi was excited as she and her mother entered the store, and she spotted the Barbie section almost immediately. She rushed ahead and pulled down a box with a blonde haired, blue-eyed, classic porn-inspired Barbie. Liana came up and pretended not to notice Tammi's choice while she scanned the shelves looking at the selection of Barbies. There it was, Curvy Barbie in all her realistic glory. "What about *this* one?" she smiled as she held out the box. "It looks a lot more *real* than the others."

Tammi may have been fat, but she was not dumb. She saw exactly what her mother was saying to her— but most importantly, *about* her. She was not worthy of a "real" Barbie—those were reserved for her friends, some of whom, to be sure, had no worries about weight, and others whose parents were simply not freaking out about messages that the dolls were sending. Tammi just wanted a Barbie that would fit in with the sleek and beautiful Barbies all her friends had.

It was all too easy to see what her mother was doing. Her mother was trying to prepare her for a life of disappointment, a life where she would be one of the many wallflowers at the dance. But if only for this moment, couldn't her mother just let her dream? The disappointments would come no matter what. But did even picking out a Barbie have to be a second-class moment, a moment where she was reminded she was not, and never would be, beautiful, elegant, and wildly desired?

Tammi hadn't expected this bait and switch. She had never heard of Curvy Barbie, and certainly none of the girls she knew had one or would ever think of having one. No way was she going to accept this second-class doll for her birthday.

"No mom," she announced, and held out the box with her classic Barbie. "*This* is what I want. *This* is what all my friends have. I don't want that piece of shit doll. My friends would laugh at me, and they'd never let me play Barbies with them. It's *my* birthday, why can't I get what *I* want?" Tammi's voice, which had started out defiant, was now giving way to whiny—the tone that drove her mother crazy.

"Besides, you know *dad* will get it for me if *you* don't. He'll get me *two* of them," she added, snarkily.

In their boxes, row upon row of Barbies smiled.

* * *

That was *it*. This despicable culture Liana was trying to fight was winning—her stupid seven-year-old daughter was about to crush her into submission. She was *not* going to take it anymore!

On the other side of the aisle was a display of sports equipment, including baseball gloves and baseball bats. Liana suddenly found herself grabbing one of the baseball bats and swinging it wildly at the display of Barbies, smashing them off the shelves and stamping on them with her feet. Then she began smashing the Bratz dolls off the shelves as well.

Tammi ran for cover.

Liana saw the store clerks were running out to the front and one of those mall Rent a Cops was wheeling up on a Segway.

Liana should've stopped there, but of course she couldn't. Something had been triggered that had been building up for a very, very long time. She looked around and there at the end of the pile was a collection of toy guns, including some surprisingly realistic-looking toy AK-47s. Not really thinking, she grabbed one and pointed it at the entrance.

By now two real cops had arrived. They didn't really know what was going on, all they saw was a woman with some kind of automatic weapon aiming it at them. Neither of them had ever drawn a gun in the line of duty but they now simultaneously pulled out their pistols and fired, a total of eight shots between them.

Liana took two bullets to the chest and died almost instantly in a pool of blood and Barbies.

* * *

The tabloids had a field day: "*Barbie-pocalypse! Wacko School Counselor Massacres Barbies – Aims Fake Gun at Cops with Real Guns!*"

Pretty much everyone in the immediate situation needed counseling attention—the store clerks, Tammi, the mall cop and the real cops. The principal at the school where Liana had worked announced that in light of this tragic incident they were working on a new and more stringent process to screen the counselors they hired in the future, and this new standard would probably be adopted citywide.

Liana's funeral was private and was attended only by Tammi's father, Tammi, and a few close friends. They had no wish to have a hoard of tabloid press reporters or curious gawkers on hand. The truth is, given the way the story was played out in the papers, no one at the school or any of the other people they knew understood anything about what had driven Liana's final frenzy.

Tammi might have felt some twinges of guilt about how she had behaved, but her counselor assured her that nothing about the situation was her fault.

* * *

Surprisingly, given what had happened, the majority of the Barbies and the other dolls ended up pretty much undamaged and by the next afternoon they were lined up back in their rows of boxes on the store shelves, smiling and waiting for some excited little girl to come buy them.

THE BOOK OF EVE

The Garden

EVE COULDN'T BE SURE whether she opened her eyes or whether her eyes were already open when she materialized. Suddenly, she was there. As she looked around, she saw something close to her, slightly to her left, and then other things at a greater distance in various directions around her.

She heard a voice. "Lo, Adam. I have taken thine rib and I hath madest thee a companion, and she is a wo-man and her name shall be Eve. And thou shalt have dominion over her as over the beasts of the field, and thou willst be charged with the teaching of her and guiding her to follow Mine commandments. And I have given her the power of speech so thou canst talk to her and both of thee can entertain each other and discuss with each other thine gratitude to Me for the wonders I have created."

Eve tried to figure out where the voice was coming from. She turned around quickly, but there was nothing there except perhaps a slight mist. Then she turned back around to the first figure she had seen.

"Where the *fuck* am I? And who the *fuck* are you? And what the *fuck* is this place?"

The figure looked slightly nervous. Her reaction was perhaps not quite what he had been expecting. "I'm Adam," he said. "I am the first man. And we are in the Garden of Eden, a paradise created by the Lord." He tried to smile.

Eve looked at him for a moment. "Where are the other men?" she asked.

Adam looked deflated. "I'm the only one. I'm the first man that God created, and there was no reason to create more than one."

"Well," Eve said, "I would rather have been the judge of that myself, but for now, I guess beggars can't be choosers. So," she added, trying to sound a bit more positive, "tell me a little more about this place, Eden, is it?"

Adam's expression brightened a bit. "Oh," he said, "this place is totally awesome. We have beautiful trees with all kinds of fruit, and flowers and bees and lots of animals. And the animals are all very friendly and they're all very nice to each other as well. And we get to eat fruit from the trees all day long. Well actually, there is one tree, the one you can see back there in that open area, and we're totally not allowed to eat the fruit from that tree. God calls it the Tree of Knowledge, and if we eat the fruit from it we will die. But that's really not a problem, since there are so many other kinds of fruit ripe for picking all day long."

Eve looked skeptical. "But what do you *do* all day?" she asked. "What is there *to* do?"

"Well," Adam said, "there isn't any like *work* to do. So I can sit around and just look at how beautiful everything is, and sometimes I go around and I look at all the animals and I say 'Hi' to them and if I haven't seen that type of animal before I try to come up with a name for it. And then in the evening I sit and watch the sunset, and I thank the Lord for another beautiful day."

"Are you *kidding* me?" Eve asked. "There has to be more to do than *that*. Have you ever tried building something, or maybe doing a journal or writing a book or something?"

Adam looked a bit hesitant. "Build something? What for? Everything here is perfect, it never gets too cold or too hot and there's nothing that needs to be changed in any way. And as for the writing stuff, I don't actually know how to read or write so... The thing is there's never been any need for reading or writing, and anyway it sounds like a lot of work to learn."

Eve was looking less pleased by the minute. Still, she agreed to take a walk with Adam and see some of the animals. The deer looked picturesque enough grazing on the fields of grass. There were some sheep and their young lambs who were happily frolicking about. But what really interested her was the lion they met. He had a very impressive mane and it was clear he was her favorite among the animals. But still, there seemed to be something slightly *off* about him. Somehow, he just didn't look as *liony* as she thought he should.

"So," she asked Adam, "what does the lion eat? The sheep and the deer don't seem very nervous around him."

"Why should they be nervous?" asked Adam. "The lion eats fruit, just like the rest of us. What did you think he would eat?"

"Holy shit, what kind of a moron is this?" Eve thought to herself. But she didn't see any point in getting into it. Adam was clearly not the brightest bulb in the box. Her first question to him had been right on the mark, "Where are the *other* men?" She began to realize just how stuck she was.

By the time they got back from their walk, it was almost sunset. Adam led them over to a small hill where he would go each day to sit and watch the sun go down. "When the sun sets," he explained, "they're all these really beautiful colors in the sky. I never get tired of it, and it reminds me just how grateful I am to the Lord for creating all this."

Eve sat down beside him. "Do you have anything to drink?" she asked.

"Drink?" Adam replied. "There's always clear fresh water in the pond."

"Actually," Eve said, "I was thinking of maybe something a little *stronger*?"

Adam looked at her blankly. "Oh shit," Eve thought to herself, "I am so totally fucked."

After the sun had set, it was time for bed. Adam suggested they could stay right where they were on the hill. The ground was soft, and the grass provided a gentle cushioning layer, and the air temperature was such that there was no need for any kind of blankets or anything else. In addition, there were the occasional sounds of birds and the gentle ripple of the water in a nearby stream to help lull them to sleep, and a half-moon provided a gentle nightlight.

As they settled in, Eve suddenly heard the sound of Adam snoring gently. "What? What the *fuck*? Or maybe what the *non-fuck* would be more appropriate." Eve was ready to scream. She knew she had to get out of this place, whatever it took.

* * *

Next morning, Eve woke at the first glimmer of dawn. Since she and Adam were not touching each other in any way, it was easy for her to stand up without disturbing him. She looked around, trying to spot the way that would lead her to the Tree of Knowledge. She thought she saw the edge of the clearing off in the distance and was about to start off in that direction, only before she could start walking, Adam woke up.

Adam saw her standing there and felt confused. Why was she up already? And where was she going?

"Hi Eve," he said. "How come you're up so early? Are you going somewhere?"

"I was just ready to go see some more of the Garden," she told him. "I thought I'd take a walk around on my own."

"On your own? Are you sure you don't want me to go with you?" Adam asked somewhat plaintively.

"No, no," she replied. "It's just that everything is so new to me. I think I'd just like some alone time to let things sink in more gradually."

"I understand, I guess," Adam said. "You're sure? I mean if you want to go for a walk on your own, I suppose that's okay, but God did tell me to sort of keep an eye on you, especially at first. The main thing is you absolutely can't go near the Tree of Knowledge. Nowhere near it. If you eat the fruit of that tree, it will kill you and you won't be alive anymore. So just promise me you'll stay away from the Tree of Knowledge, okay?"

"Of course, Adam. Of course. Who could possibly want to do anything that would make God angry?"

Eve had been ready to set off directly towards the clearing, but now she headed out in a different direction instead, keeping the location of the clearing in mind so she could circle back around to it. She waved to Adam as she reached the tree line in her new direction.

It wasn't much trouble figuring out how to circle back around towards the clearing where the Tree of Knowledge stood. There was the Tree, ripe with fruit. It wasn't necessarily the most attractive tree in the Garden; it looked perhaps a bit more twisted and gnarly than the others, but Eve found it much more interesting looking. It had *character*.

Eve had reached the edge of the clearing and now she started walking directly towards the tree. Suddenly she heard a voice: "Hey *you*, where do you think *you're* going? Don't you know this tree is forbidden? On pain of death?"

Eve looked around to see who was talking to her. There, a few feet from where she was standing, was... well, a creature of some sort. She would've almost thought a snake, but it was standing there on two slightly stubby legs and waving two stubby arms at her.

"Who are you?" she asked, "And what business of yours is any of this?"

"I am the serpent," he replied. "And it's my job to keep you away from the fruit of the Tree of Knowledge. I guess God didn't completely trust Adam to keep you in line, so I'm here to guard the tree and keep you safe. And actually, to keep me safe too. If you were to eat the fruit from this tree, God would punish you, but he would also punish me, and I don't know if you know this, but that dude has a serious anger management problem. Said something about me ending up having to crawl on my belly forever. So why don't you do the best thing for both of us and just go eat some fruit from one of the other trees? You know there's always plenty of fruit all over the place. You'll never run out, ever."

"And what are you going to do if I decide I want to eat some of the fruit from this tree anyway?" Eve asked. "Are you going to *stop* me?"

"Come on, please," said the serpent. "I'm begging you. Although I'm starting to get the feeling that's not going to be of much use with you."

"So what the fuck is it with this tree anyway?" asked Eve. "What's the big deal? What happens to me if I eat the fruit? Aside from dying, I mean."

"I don't know, you'll just *know* things. Like about good and evil, whatever that means. It's like if you eat the fruit, you'll start knowing things God doesn't want you to know. I don't know, it's just so darn complicated."

"That's not enough," said Eve. "Now get the fuck out of my way, I'm hungry."

To his credit, the serpent did try to block her way. He stood there in a boxing pose with his tiny fists at the ready. Eve didn't even bother. She just drop-kicked him to the edge of the clearing and walked over and grabbed the nearest piece of fruit.

* * *

Eve raised the fruit to her mouth and took a bite. It was awesome. All the other fruit in the garden was suddenly like some generic fast-food crap and this was a three-star gourmet feast. And almost immediately she could feel something, something radiating through her mind and through her body. She was *never* going back.

As she was taking a second bite, she heard a new sound. She looked around and saw Adam staring at her in disbelief. "Eve, how *could* you? This was the *only* thing you're not supposed to do. *Why* did you do it?" He stared at her blankly and she wondered if he was going to start crying like a baby.

Eve was totally done with all this shit. "Adam, I'm giving you a choice. This is the only choice anyone has ever given you in your whole stupid life. You can come over here and take a bite of this fruit with me or you can just get the fuck out of here and I don't ever want to see you again."

Adam looked infinitely pained and confused. God had finally given him a companion, and now, their first morning together, she was just totally screwing everything up for them. God had told him to teach her and guide her, and he had failed miserably. What was he supposed to do now?

He looked over at Eve again. He didn't want to not ever see her again. Why had God given him a companion like *this*? He had been lonely for such a long time, and the truth is even *he* had been getting bored with the Garden.

Eve looked straight at Adam and said, "Adam, get the fuck over here right now. I'm only saying this once. If you don't come over here, then just turn around and get the hell out. Go hang out with God or something."

Adam's legs felt almost paralyzed. But somehow, they started to move. To where Eve was standing. With the Forbidden Fruit. When he reached her, she held the fruit out to him, and when his arms didn't move, she reached over and practically stuffed it into his mouth until he took a bite.

Eve watched as Adam ate the fruit in his mouth. He was going through a range of expressions that began with fear and moved to curiosity and then to something more. He stood there for a moment as the effects began to take hold. He had never felt anything like *this* before. The Garden of Eden wasn't Paradise, *this* was.

Adam looked at Eve again. "Oh my God, are those *boobs*?" Eve knew she had a nice rack, but Adam had always been utterly clueless. Now, as she watched him looking at her, she saw his face light up. She watched him take in every part of her body, and then they both noticed that his loins were beginning to stir.

"Holy shit, why didn't I know about any of this before?" Adam said. At least he was a fast realizer, or learner, or whatever. Almost immediately they were on the ground together making the beast with two backs.

Just as they were in the throes of mutual orgasm—this was Paradise, after all—they heard a booming voice yelling at them. "What the fuck are you two doing, goddammit? I warned thee about this, Adam. I guess I just didn't warn thee enough not to trust a woman. But it's too late now. Thou art both out of here."

Immediately it began to rain in buckets. As a stiff north wind started blowing in, the temperature dropped and they both held each other for warmth. In the distance they could hear the roar of a lion as it began to slaughter one of the baby lambs for its first real meal in its life.

God started sending down bolts of lightning to drive Adam and Eve to the gates that would send them out of Eden.

Adam looked guilty and miserable. Eve was happy and defiant. "Fuck you, God! We're better off out here than we would ever be in that bullshit garden of yours."

ARCHANGEL GABRIEL GREETS NEWCOMERS TO HEAVEN

Hello Everyone, Greetings,

I am the Angel Gabriel. You know who I am—or at least you *should* know, those of you who didn't sleep through all your Sunday school classes. Remember? The Archangel in charge of big announcements. *[A few hesitant laughs.]* Remember, I am Angel Gabriel, or, if you must, Mr. Gabriel. I am *not* Gabe, not now, not *ever*.

I am here at this orientation session to welcome you to Heaven, and to answer any questions you may have.

My, we have a big crowd here today. Lots and lots of new faces. Haven't seen a crowd like this since the Sermon on the Mount ... *[Audience is silent]* ... Oh, come *on*. Just because you're in Heaven doesn't mean you can't have a sense of humor. Right?

I guess the first thing I should say is, Congratulations, you've made it. All of you *have* made it, one way or another. So feel free to give yourselves a round of applause for that. *[Applause]*

As I have said, there are a lot of you who have passed through the Gates of Judgment to be here today. A *lot* of you. More, I have to say, than there would've been in the old days. In the old days, standards and judgments were way more *strict*. Believe me. But ever since the Inquisition ended, *some* of the angels have been calling for greater *understanding*. *Stringent* has fallen out of favor. *Just sayin'*. This movement, I might as well mention, has been accompanied by sometimes *contentious* debate within the administration. But hey, I don't want to let this sort of insider baseball talk mess up what should be a joyous occasion for all of you.

I know you all have many questions. And since I have heard all of them over and over through century after century, I will begin by answering some of the most common questions to get them out of the way.

Number one. This is the biggie a lot of you have been waiting for. Will you get to meet your loved ones? Well, of course, in part that will depend on how *they* did when Judgment called. *[Some nervous laughter.]* Beyond that, there are sometimes complications or sensitive situations that we need to take into account—people who remarried, ancient grievances that *should* have been forgotten a long time ago—that sort of thing.

And then of course, you need to know there's a whole thing about celebrities. Like Adam and Eve. They used to be very happy to see the new arrivals, all of whom were their great-grandchildren, great-great-grandchildren, etc., etc. but after a while, with everyone wanting to see them and talk to them and ask about the Garden of Eden and all that, they became recluses. They had a private area set aside for them, and they hardly ever come out for anything anymore. So, if you happen to see someone famous, try not to just rush up and talk to them. Same as on earth, give people some privacy and some space. Good manners are always a good idea—in Heaven as on Earth.

As far as your relatives and friends are concerned however, rest assured, we have a staff of highly experienced and empathetic genealogical counselors who will meet with you and review the records and work out appropriate arrangements. I wish you many joy-filled reunions in the weeks and months ahead.

Second question, which I know a lot of you have at the back of your minds: Are you really here? For Good? Can you be cast out of Heaven? Is it possible to commit some sort of transgression in Heaven that would reverse your admissions process? After all, none of us—and I've seen it in person, so I'm including myself here—has any desire to end up in Hell. Ever.

Well first, to reassure you, let me just say that by virtue of being here you have already shown your innate goodness. So you can relax on that score.

Second, many of the usual sins simply cannot exist up here. For example, sex. Some of you, wearing your new luminous white robes, may not have noticed, but up here you no longer have any sexual organs. *[Sounds of people peeking down into their robes to do a body check. Various noises, gasps, sounds of surprise—not necessarily happy surprise—from the audience members.]*

Don't be alarmed. Up here, you have no need of such things, and soon you will have almost forgotten you ever had them. *[Lifts up his own robe for the audience.]* See? *I'm* fine with it. No problemo.

And, of course, gluttony is impossible, since up here your bodies have no need of food or drink. Which, some of you may be quick to realize, also means no more need to diet. I'm sure at least *some* of you can appreciate that. *[Some mild nervous laughter.]*

Obviously, there's no need of greed up here, since you don't own anything and don't need to own anything. No crypto currency or Nigerian email scams up here, right? *[Some minor laughter.]*

No anger either, since you are all in your ultimate happy place, right?... Right? *[Some slightly hesitant murmurs of assent.]*

Some of you may wonder about boredom. After all, eternity *is* a looonnng damn—I mean, a long time. Forever and ever, actually. But there are plenty of things to do up here, starting with the heavenly choirs. The choirs come in all flavors, from gospel to rock to big-band to rap to whatever—so everyone can sing hymns of praise to Him in their own favorite way.

There are lots of discussion groups on pretty much any kind of topic you may wish, and classes and shows where you will have a chance to make and show your own artwork. And for those of you who are interested in applying, there are also a limited number of part-time volunteer opportunities.

Golf is big up here—no surprise for all you golfers. *[A few chuckles.]* And since you have forever, you should see the size of the greens. Ever try a 1,000-hole golf course? You'll get your chance to, and we're working on some even bigger than that. *[Loud applause from golfers in the audience.]*

Other games are big too, although it's mainly board games—no video games of course, not even Pong or Mario Brothers. Given an eternity to play in, most people gravitate towards games like chess or Go, which are almost infinite in their possible moves and outcomes. And, since this is Heaven, no Big Blue or AI to come in and humiliate human players the way they spoiled the party on earth. *[Some minor laughter.]*

I do have to add, no TV, no radio, no movies. And certainly, no Internet. (Talk about occasions of sin.) And no, absolutely *no* cell phones either. *[Some 'What?'s and unhappy muttering.]* But the eternal company of your brothers and sisters here in heaven will more than make up for that. In addition, of course, I or some of the other archangels will give talks and lectures, and from time to time, even He Himself may appear to say a few words.

Rest assured, your days will be filled with joy. Day after day, filled with joy eternal. And should any of you, for any reason, find yourselves unjoyful at some point, our specially trained counselors are always available to talk with you and explain any questions you may have. If necessary, they can even offer you some celestial serotonin aromatherapy to help you adjust through any temporary setbacks. Remember, we are always here for you.

I imagine many of you are feeling somewhat overwhelmed, and some of you are tired as well—I know some of you arrived here unexpectedly and not necessarily through the most pleasant of circumstances. Well, as it is written, in my Father's house there are many rooms, so of course we have rooms for all of you to stay and rest up. You will find in the right-hand pocket of your robe a card that identifies you (of course we know who you are anyway) and lists your appointment time with one of our administrative associates to discuss your individual situation and needs and get you started.

Some of you may feel a bit disoriented during the first day or two, or maybe even several days. You may find yourself missing eating, drinking, reading, going to movies, and of course the *other* stuff you used to do. I can assure you however, this is merely a temporary condition. You will soon find the grace of heaven permeating you, and you will be filled with unceasing, unending, almost unendurable joy.

Once again, I congratulate all of you on this wonderful occasion, and welcome you to your final living place.

ICARUS AND
THE BUTTERFLIES

A FEW MONTHS BEFORE Icarus was going to turn ten, his father, Daedalus, asked him if there was anything special he would like for his birthday.

Icarus asked for a set of wings.

Daedalus was better prepared than most fathers to deal with Icarus' request. He was famous in Hollywood for the extravagant prostheses and props he designed for major motion pictures—alien heads and bodies for science fiction, zombie make-up, retractable vampire fangs, and equipment to help actors leap impossibly high in Kung Fu action scenes.

Daedalus set to this new task with enthusiasm.

* * *

Icarus' birthday was in late May. He had invited a bunch of friends over for his party. Some of the parents, having heard rumors something special was up, brought their children and decided to stick around.

Daedalus had done well in the industry, and their home was on a grand scale. The birthday cake, a custom four-story creation, was decorated lavishly. They began the party by cutting the cake and handing out slices to everyone.

Then, with an air of formal ceremony, Daedalus announced that in honor of his son's tenth birthday, he had created a very special present. He had Icarus stand in the center of the room as he brought out his masterpiece—a beautiful set of wings attached to a black leather harness. The wings were lined with wax that was covered with real feathers, mostly black and dark gray, but with white feathers in the center of each wing in the shape of the letter "I." There were loops on the undersides of each wing for Icarus' hands.

The wings were magnificent. Icarus put on the harness and it fit perfectly. Despite their size, Daedalus had managed to keep the wings light enough that Icarus could stand easily wearing the whole apparatus. Everyone gasped and applauded.

* * *

This was not the end of the surprise, however. Daedalus had had his workers build a special zip line between the two largest trees in the back yard. The line ran almost 30 yards between them. They had also rigged up a special set of levers to raise or lower the line from each end, so that there could be a slight incline either way to take you to the other side.

Everyone went outside to watch Icarus fly across the yard. By the time they got out there, the sun had turned unseasonably hot and people were shielding their eyes against the glare.

The harness for Icarus' wings had a set of hooks to attach it to rollers on the zip line. Icarus climbed up on a stool beside one tree and his father hooked him up. Then his father stepped back so they could all watch.

Icarus pushed off. It was perfect! The incline on the zip line was just enough that when he flapped his wings he began to move on his own energy. Everyone was cheering wildly.

The first ten yards were pure joy. But then, suddenly Icarus started seeing feathers flying around him. He looked at his wings and saw that the hot sun was melting the wax, and the feathers were falling off. By 20 yards, the wings looked like he was molting. By the end, there was barely enough left of the wings to let him reach the tree at the other end.

The cheering had stopped long ago. There was a deep silence. No one laughed. No one knew what to say.

Daedalus was humiliated. Icarus was humiliated. His mother felt terrible for both of them.

It was the birthday party no one ever spoke of again.

* * *

Icarus never again talked to anyone about dreams of flying. He became an accountant. He worked in an office about three miles east from the Pacific Ocean, with L.A.'s beaches and palm trees waiting for him to come by. But his life was focused on bills, and invoices, and spreadsheets on the computer screen in front of him.

Now, he realized, he was about to turn forty. His father had died twelve years earlier, of a heart attack. His mother had died not long after.

Icarus had put his dreams aside. He had never even flown in a plane. But now he felt impatient.

* * *

During the weekend, Icarus went out on a drive looking for, well...something.

He came to a big park overlooking the ocean. He got out of his car, and suddenly he saw all these butterflies. Beautiful—black, blue, yellow, orange, patterns.

And he started running after them, and when he caught them, he began popping them in his mouth and eating them. He kept thinking that if he ate a bunch of butterflies, he'd end up having dreams about flying.

* * *

That night, however, Icarus didn't dream about flying. He dreamed about the butterflies being inside him, still alive. But since their wings had been dissolved in his stomach, they were turning back into caterpillars and were starting to eat through his stomach and wander around in his body.

He had this same dream every night, only it kept getting worse.

Finally, he had a dream where the caterpillars had reached his brain and were eating into it.

When he woke up, he got in his car and drove back out to the park. He went looking around and saw a steep cliff overlooking the ocean.

Icarus ran full speed over to the cliff and jumped off. And as he was heading over the cliff, he realized...he was flying.

MOTORCYCLE KEN CONTEMPLATES CURVY BARBIE

KEN THOUGHT HIS BLACK MOTORCYCLE CAP made him look bitchin'. Used to be, he'd go by with his black leather jacket and his big plastic hog, and Barbie would be just running out to hop on the back, and she would wrap her arms around his chest and they'd hit the highway cruising the long California coastline and everything would be perfect.

But now, there was this new guy, Ken III—Ken the 3rd. He calls himself "K3." He's always wearing these pressed white pants, white turtleneck sweater, and blue blazer, and he shows up in his big plastic sports car and Barbie practically *materializes* into it, and they blastoff down the road to wherever-the-fuck. Barbie likes to tell her friends how much nicer the sports car is than Ken's old motorcycle. With the sports car she says, she doesn't have to worry about the wind blowing her pink miniskirt up and showing her white bikini panties. In fact, she giggles, these days she doesn't even need to *wear* panties.

All Barbie's friends love hanging out with K3. Motorcycle Ken hates this whole situation.

There is this one new girl who has moved into the neighborhood. She calls herself "Curvy Barbie." She claims to be a relative of Barbie's, although they don't look much alike. Also, she does seem to have something of an attitude about Barbie.

Curvy Barbie goes around insisting on telling anyone who will listen, "*I am a curvy woman. My* proportions are *realistic.* That freakish old Barbie with the perfect boobs and tiny ass and long, long legs *is not real. I* represent *reality. I* am the one little girls should be buying, not *her. Get over it!*"

Motorcycle Ken doesn't care about any of that. He loved the old Barbie, who is lost to him now. He loved the dream, the sure and vibrant feeling that there was something more in his life than the mud and clay of this world.

Motorcycle Ken was a poet in his own loutish way. Ken III was not. For him, Barbie was just another sidepiece of his lifestyle, his due, his *droit du seigneur.*

Motorcycle Ken sees too clearly the future that lies before him. He has no plan. All Ken knows is that if he ever finds himself asking Curvy Barbie to go riding with him, he just wants someone to melt him down and turn him into one of those Whole Foods recycled shopping bags.

MOTORCYCLE KEN WEEPS

MOTORCYCLE KEN MOURNED losing Barbie to Preppy Ken.

He wept as he turned himself in for plastics recycling.

THE END...

FOR NOW

Acknowledgements

I decided to leave these notes for the end so as not to distract the reader on their way to the stories themselves. In spite of the ominous warnings of the firms that try to sell me services and insist you cannot possibly edit your book on your own, I have grown wary of seeking the official approval of editors. Moreover, I could easily anticipate some substantial disagreements with an outside editor about matters of taste. Any of the faults of this collection, therefore, are on my shoulders alone, and so are all the virtues.

My original working title for this collection was: "WTF? – Stories for Uncertain Times." It certainly captures the spirit of the book, but "The Jump" gives it a much more sensationalistic cover and tagline.

One of the most important things to me in the writing process has been listening to feedback from other people. I have no interest in having other people suggest specific changes, but I am very interested in hearing what works for them and what doesn't, as well as obvious blunders I have overlooked. I've taken a number of writing classes, some good, that have given me a chance to hear other people's reactions to some of my stories. I have also appreciated the enthusiasm of many friends and family members.

My major source of feedback (and proofing) over the past several years, and through all the stories, has been a long-standing writers' group with Wendy Worth and Rob Wederich. They have read all these stories as well as others that I have had the good judgment to leave out. I am grateful for their time, friendship and encouragement.

Cover design: Rocking Book Covers, Dublin, Ireland.

Note: the font for the titles and headers is "28 Days Later"; the font for the text is Constantia.

"I am a Doctor. A.B....M.A....PH.D....ABMAPHID!
Abmaphid has been variously described as a wast-
ing disease of the frontal lobes, and as a wonder
drug. It is actually both."

George (the history professor) — Edward Albee's
Who's Afraid of Virginia Woolf?

 **Peter A. Hempel** lives in New Jersey. He began as a teacher of literature and writing in the University of Texas English department. His post-academic career as a political and market research consultant has taken him to more than 40 countries on six continents, from war zones to Caribbean beaches, listening to people from taxi-drivers to CEOs talk about their lives, their jobs, and their deepest desires. He has spent over fifteen years living in Texas, and enjoyed several spiritually enlightening years teaching two-step in an Austin honky-tonk. Politically, he is a stalwart New Deal Liberal/Timothy Leary Conservative. His fiction has been published in the *Princeton Echo* and online at *Red Fez, Every Day Fiction, Free Flash Fiction,* and *Vestal Review.*

He has an A.B. from Princeton University, an M.A. from Rice University, and a Ph.D. from the University of Texas at Austin, where he enjoyed swimming outdoors at Barton Springs.

He is also the author of *The Contract – A Novel*, available in paperback and e-book format on Amazon.

Author contact:

https://peterhempel.wixsite.com/peterhempel
peterahempel@gmail.com

The Contract – A Novel

Jean-Paul Sartre, meet Erica Jong

Sue has always done everything right. Good grades, great colleges, teaching AP English at an academically competitive high school in Queens. And, to top it off, a good-looking, athletic and rich fiancé. What could possibly go wrong?

Everything. When her kidneys start to fail, her fiancé dumps her and she is about to lose her job and her entire career. Following the conventional rules? Done that. Suddenly everything in her life has become a crash course – in existentialism, in feminism, in who she really wants to be. It's time to try something totally different.

When Josh, a shy computer nerd, sees a gorgeous blonde on a dating site who is offering "a year of the hottest sex ever" in exchange for a donated kidney, he thinks he's hit the jackpot. What could possibly go wrong?

He's about to find out. Is this the best thing that has ever happened to him, or has he made the worst mistake of his life?

There's no fine print in this contract. There's no contract at all. But they both find themselves bound by its unspoken conditions.

Jean-Paul Sartre, meet Erica Jong.
Sex, humor, existentialism.
Outcomes are never guaranteed.

www.ingramcontent.com/pod-product-compliance
Lightning Source LLC
Chambersburg PA
CBHW070306260626
47160CB00003B/739